I0762748

## Advance Praise for *Smash or Pass*

"*Smash or Pass* is an ace of a book. Birdie Schae perfectly captures the magic of summer camp, all while serving up a sweet sapphic romance with friendships (and older brothers!) that you'll fall for just as much as the love story."

—Rachael Lippincott, #1 *New York Times* bestselling author of *Five Feet Apart*

"Pure sunshine filtered through the lens of an earnest autistic teenager. Schae has written a sweet, tenderhearted story of reclaiming your identity and finding the people meant for you."

—Kelly Quindlen, bestselling author of *She Drives Me Crazy*

"*Smash or Pass* is an adorable, enchanting story about finding love, finding community, and finding yourself. Anyone who's ever found the truest version of themselves in spaces made for them will see themselves in these lovable characters. Gooey, sweet, and feel-good in the best way."

—Sophie Gonzales, international bestselling author of *If This Gets Out*

"Pure fun! Birdie Schae has written a charming rom-com with nostalgic summer vibes and a heartfelt emotional journey. You can't help but root for Ellie as she falls in love with Sierra—and learns to love herself, too."

—Ann Zhao, indie bestselling author of *Dear Wendy*

"Much like the protagonist of this heartfelt, effervescent debut, I also have seven rules that I live by, and I'll share them with you now. Rule #1: Read *Smash or Pass* immediately. Rules #2–6: Reread *Smash or Pass* immediately. Rule #7: Thank Birdie Schae for writing an absolute treasure of a novel."

—Erin Baldwin, author of *Wish You Weren't Here*

"Birdie Schae's debut feels like sunshine and coming home. The warmth of *Heartstopper* meets a whirlwind summer camp setting. *Smash or Pass* is a vibrant, funny, poignant joy with a swoony, sapphic love story."

—Kalie Holford, author of *The Last Love Song*

"*Smash or Pass* is a book that feels just like first love. You truly feel for and root for each character in equal measure. This book is an absolute smash!"

—SAMANTHA MARKUM, *USA Today* bestselling author of *Love, Off the Record*

"A sparkling sapphic debut, *Smash or Pass* serves up a slow-burn, teammates-to-lovers romance as warm as the beach on a summer day. Achingly heartfelt, deeply tender, and an incredibly necessary addition to the 'helping your totally platonic crush apply sunscreen while trying really hard to be cool about it' literary canon."

—JENNA VORIS, author of *Every Time You Hear That Song* and *Say a Little Prayer*

"Full of warmth and light, *Smash or Pass* is a cozy summer campfire in book form. A sweet, authentic debut novel that inspires self-acceptance and healing, with a tender sapphic romance to cheer on from the sidelines."

—CL MONTBLANC, author of *Pride or Die*

"Tender, funny, and heartwarming, *Smash or Pass* is all of the sweetest parts of summer and first love rolled into one triumphant romance."

—ELLE GONZALEZ ROSE, author of *Marisol Acts the Part*

"I wish I could spend every summer in the sands of *Smash or Pass* with its roster of witty, bighearted characters. Do not pass; Schae's sporty and sincere debut is a total winner."

—JEN ST. JUDE, author of *If Tomorrow Doesn't Come*

"A warm embrace of a book that deftly explores self-acceptance, the families we find, and the love that finds us."

—SUJIN WITHERSPOON, author of *Bingsu for Two*

"A sweet coming-of-age romance about the safe spaces we find with people who see us—and love us—for exactly who we are."

—ELLEN O'CLOVER, author of *Seven Percent of Ro Devereux*

"Full of heart and fun in the sun, *Smash or Pass* serves up a diverse coming-of-age story about friendship, self-discovery, and first love—on and off the court."

—SYDNEY LANGFORD, author of *Someone to Daydream About*

# Smash or Pass

BIRDIE SCHAE

ALFRED A. KNOPF
New York

A Borzoi Book published by Alfred A. Knopf
An imprint of Random House Children's Books
A division of Penguin Random House LLC
1745 Broadway, New York, NY 10019
penguinrandomhouse.com
rhcbooks.com



Editor: Marisa DiNovis
Cover Designer: Michelle Cunningham
Interior Designer: Michelle Gengaro-Kokmen
Production Editor: Melinda Ackell
Managing Editor: Jake Eldred
Production Manager: Tracy Heydweiller

Library of Congress Cataloging-in-Publication Data is available upon request.
ISBN 979-8-217-03326-3 (trade) — ISBN 979-8-217-03328-7 (ebook)

The text of this book is set in 11-point Warnock Pro Regular.

Manufactured in the United States of America
1st Printing

The authorized representative in the EU for product safety and compliance is Penguin Random House Ireland, Morrison Chambers, 32 Nassau Street, Dublin D02 YH68, Ireland, https://eu-contact.penguin.ie.

*To Miro, who always made summer camp feel all the more special. I can't imagine a better friend to have spent those eight summers with.*

*And to everyone who has ever been deemed too much. You are the exact right amount, and I love you.*

# 1. Never Get in a Car with Your Boyfriend

Whenever I enter my therapist's office, she makes me rate my emotions on a scale from one to ten. It can be about anything—from my level of stress about a certain situation to how happy I've been feeling lately—and though I thought it was too childish for a sixteen-year-old at first, I've grown used to the question over time. So much that even right now, weeks away from our next appointment, I can hear her voice in my head.

*On a scale from one to ten, how upset does this make you?*

The answer comes to me easily, but it can't possibly be true. Because something tells me that my boyfriend breaking up with me isn't supposed to feel like a mere four.

"Listen, Ellie, I just don't think this is going to work," Daniel tells me while I sit there, frozen in his passenger seat, repeating his words in my head for the fifth time. I wait and wait and wait for my heart to break, for that horrible, sinking feeling in my chest, but even as the houses and lampposts outside the car keep flashing by, nothing really happens. The world around me doesn't come crashing down. I don't start crying. But Daniel?

He sighs.

"This doesn't have to be some big deal, you know," he says, looking at me expectantly, but I still can't will my lips to part.

See, this is exactly why I have to stick to my rules at all times. Those seven simple bullet points I wrote down right before the start of high school are the whole reason people in this town like me, and they have never once failed me since I began to follow them religiously three years ago. If I had just stuck to them like I normally do, I wouldn't be in this situation at all because of *Rule #1: Try to avoid one-on-one conversations and stay in groups as much as possible. That way, before you react to something someone says, you can quickly look around and make sure you act the way you're expected to.*

I knew better than to get into this car all alone with Daniel, but . . . I don't know. I guess he was so insistent on driving me to Blake's party that I let myself be naive for a second, wanting to believe that one little exception on our six-month anniversary couldn't hurt.

I was wrong.

"Just because I'm breaking up with you doesn't mean we have to start acting all weird," Daniel continues. "We can just go to this party and explain to our friends that we decided to end things, and then we can move on with our lives like nothing ever happened between us." He shrugs. "I mean, I see no reason for us to stop being friends."

What he's saying makes perfect sense, except for the fact

that Daniel and I have never actually *been* friends. We were strangers who hung out with each other because of our newly intertwined friend groups, and then, exactly six months ago, we started kissing each other. Nothing less, nothing more.

I don't say any of that, though. I don't think Daniel would appreciate me disagreeing with him on whether we have a friendship we can return to or not. The only issue is that I don't know what he *does* want to hear right now, even though I did follow *Rule #2: Before you meet up with people, take some time to prepare yourself for possible scenarios.*

I spent over half an hour making sure I'd know what to do in case any of the situations I could think of become a reality tonight. I prepared myself for my friends getting a little too drunk and practiced what to say if we play spin the bottle and I am expected to kiss someone who isn't Daniel. I even looked up what to do if my brother and my best friend start dating, even though one thing is for sure: That will *never* happen, no matter what Nina believes.

The possibility of my boyfriend breaking up with me, however? It never once crossed my mind.

There's not much time left to dwell on how incredibly unprepared I am for this, though. We turn another corner in silence, now less than a minute away from Blake's party, and since there's no way for me to subtly pull out my phone and read a detailed guide to breakups right now, I have no choice but to say the first thing that comes to mind.

"If that's what you want, then I guess we should just . . . stay friends."

My words have barely had time to turn cold in the air between us when the car comes to a stop. Daniel turns to me immediately, scanning my face with those blue eyes I've grown familiar with over the past few months. There's a frown between his brows, and he blinks once, twice, thrice before finally seeming to realize that I'm not going to burst into tears or slap him in the face.

He swallows, his jaw set. "Wait, so . . . no hard feelings between us, then?"

"No hard feelings," I repeat with a single nod. For a moment, I think that maybe we should shake hands on it, make it official, but I ultimately decide against it. Only a few seconds later, the two of us leave the car—and each other—behind.

Teenage life usually follows a pattern, and as I enter Blake's party, I'm glad the rest of the night seems to be falling right into it. Dozens of groups have already claimed their spots across the room, some people leaning against the walls with their hands wrapped around their cups while others have decided to settle on the floor instead of the empty couch they're literally resting their backs against. There are even a few people who have gathered on the staircase, of all places.

It's scarily familiar, as if somebody copy-pasted the scene in front of me from my memories of last week's party. And the one before that. And all the other ones I've gone to, actually.

I was fourteen the first time Nina insisted I come along with her to one of Blake's parties, so now, over two years and approximately too many long nights later, it's not that hard for me to guess what tonight will end up looking like. People will get way too drunk, we'll play stupid games even though we know they always end up causing drama, a few people will hook up, and by the next morning our whole school will have heard about everything that went down.

There should be no more surprises tonight. Which is exactly how I like it.

My eyes roam around the room in hopes of finding a white girl with blond hair, and . . . well, there are quite a lot of those, actually, but none of them are Nina Davis. So I keep walking.

I scan as many faces as possible while making my way through the groups of friends, but everything quickly starts to blur together. Shoulders bump into mine, the smell of alcohol gets heavier the deeper I go into the dancing crowd, and voices surround me until there's not even an inch of space left for me to simply *breathe.*

The world around me spins out of focus. It's too much, too much, *too much,* and yet everything seems so far away. As if I'm not really here. As if I'm merely a ghost moving through this room of things that should be tangible but only leave me with a numb kind of tingling when I reach out.

That is, until I feel a firm tug on my arm.

"Hello? Earth to Ellie?" Nina tries, snapping her fingers in front of my face until I've returned to the world of the living. She's straightened her blond hair so it falls perfectly over her exposed shoulders. The light blue denim top she's wearing is absolutely stunning, hugging her body in all the right places and revealing how her normally pale white skin has tanned. I would ask her where she bought it if it weren't for the fact that, unlike Nina, even the Florida sun can't make me look less white. Wearing pastel colors makes me feel like I'm a walking bottle of milk.

I usually stick to warm shades, like the off-the-shoulder red top I'm wearing right now, which I combined with my jean shorts that have little roses embroidered on them.

I only realize I've just been wordlessly staring at her when Nina crosses her arms over her chest and tells me, "You're scaring me. You good?"

*Get yourself together, Eleanore.*

"Sorry, sorry," I say quickly. "I'm fine. Just . . . having a moment."

Nina nods, but she eyes me in that way that makes me feel small, despite us being the same height. I almost think she's going to tell me to never have a "moment" again, but instead she sighs. "Whatever." Then her eyes move on to look around the room. "Where's Daniel? Aren't you two supposed to be all cutesy while celebrating right now?"

*Oh. Right.*

"Well, about that," I start, my heart beating ten times faster than it did while I was in Daniel's car. With a curious eyebrow raised at me, Nina lifts her cup of beer to her mouth, and I can't help but look down at the basic white sneakers on my feet before ripping off the Band-Aid. "We broke up, actually."

"YOU WHAT?!" Nina exclaims, almost choking on her drink in the process. I let her cough a few times before explaining.

"It happened, like, ten minutes ago." I give my best attempt at a casual shrug before I add, "I was going to tell you as soon as I could, which is, well, right now. But I'm fine. Honestly. It's not a big deal."

I've barely said it before the ever-present voice in my head reminds me of *Rule #3: Repeat things in your head before you say them out loud, and always add enough clarity so your words can't be misunderstood.*

And so I continue talking, just to make sure she understands. "I mean, it's not a big deal as in there are no hard feelings between us. We just came to the conclusion that the two of us weren't really working together and that we'd be better off as friends, so nothing will actually have to change." I pause. "Except for the part where we kiss and hold hands, of course. That will definitely change since—"

"I get it, Ellie," Nina interrupts before putting her hand on my shoulder and squeezing gently. "I'm glad we're still good to hang out with him and the other boys, but that doesn't make this any less heartbreaking! I really thought you and Daniel were going to be in love forever." She sighs, shaking her head slowly.

"Let's look at it from the bright side," I say, swallowing hard. "At least now I won't have to go to that summer camp with him. I'm sure my parents can still cancel, which means I'll have a whole lot more time to do fun things with you instead!"

When Daniel asked me to join him at a beach volleyball camp called SMASH! a few months ago and I said yes, Nina was upset we'd have less time to spend with each other this summer. So much so that she even considered coming along herself, though that might have had to do with my brother being a SMASHER!—his words, not mine—too. Ultimately, though, the thought of, and I quote, "sweating and rolling around in the sand" was a big enough dealbreaker for Nina to not want to go.

"So I'm your second choice for summer plans?" she teases now, but the smile quickly fades from her face, turning into a groan. "I need another drink to process this news."

Before I know it, Nina has not only grabbed herself a new beer but pushed one into my hands as well.

"Thanks," I force out before taking the tiniest sip known to humankind. Either there is more wrong with me than I originally thought, or people who say you get used to the taste of beer are all liars. Because even after trying it at various parties, I still have to use all my willpower to keep the disgust off my face.

I can't be seen as that one boring girl who refuses to drink, though. So, at each party, I let people offer me one drink and then spend the rest of the night holding on to that very same cup, occasionally bringing it to my lips but never getting close to finishing it. The illusion that I'm drinking is all it takes for people to leave me alone.

I guess that's the thing about fitting in. The key to it isn't to be exactly like everyone else. It's just to make them believe you are. In all the right ways, at least.

"God, I just can't wrap my head around the fact that you guys broke up. Romance is officially dead to me," Nina declares after downing half her drink. She taps her cup against my full one, giving me a small smile. "The only love I'll ever need is your friendship. Who needs boys when we have each other, right?"

Warmth gathers in my chest at her words, and I'm about to

tell her *I sure don't* when she adds, "Though I'm also here if you do want to rant about boys, of course."

She looks at me expectantly, eyebrows raised slightly as she waits for me to take her up on that offer. But I won't, which she should know by now. After all, talking about how I'm feeling isn't exactly a good idea with the existence of *Rule #4: Always keep the topic of the conversation on the other person. If you start rambling about things you feel strongly about, you won't know when or how to shut up.*

I clear my throat, trying to come up with a new topic of conversation that Nina will find interesting enough to drop this without thinking twice. Preferably one that does not revolve around my brother.

I fail.

"About you wanting to give up on romance, though . . . if I were you, I'd reconsider," I tell Nina. As soon as the words are out, I'm already regretting every single life decision that has led me here, to this exact moment. "I overheard Noah talking to one of his summer camp friends on the phone. Apparently he regrets not asking a girl out in the past, so he said that if he has another shot with her, he definitely won't make the same mistake again."

A smile slowly creeps onto Nina's face, getting brighter and brighter every second until she's practically glowing, lighting up the room in a way that the cheap disco lights can only dream of.

"I knew it!" she says. "Oh my god. We've been sitting next to each other in history for so long, but lately something has just . . . *changed* between us. He's constantly trying to find an excuse to talk to me now."

She grabs my hand excitedly, telling me about all the things they've been talking about during class. One thing is for sure: We are *not* passing the Bechdel test tonight.

While Nina rambles on and on, I make sure I don't forget about *Rule #5: Make eye contact when people talk so they know you're listening to them. If they're talking about how they are feeling, nod so they know you think their feelings are valid. Don't forget to smile casually if it's a lighter topic.*

Right now that means forcing the corners of my mouth to lift, hoping my smile doesn't falter as I listen to Nina thirst after my twin brother. Aside from the fact that it's weird as hell to hear this, I generally don't like giving my best friend hope when I know for a fact that my brother doesn't like her at all—especially not in a romantic way. Even though we barely speak to each other nowadays, that much is clear.

Although it *is* strange that he's been talking to Nina at all . . .

My best friend is still rambling when Blake jumps on a table and cups his hands around his mouth to yell, "May I have your attention, people!" Conversations all around us pause as pretty much everyone turns to him, almost like he's some sort of god.

That might not even be that far off—at least, if a god of alcohol exists. Blake and his older brother have been hosting Willowmoor High's parties and sneaking in drinks since my first year of high school, though Blake's legacy is now nearing its end. After being held back for two years, this is finally the summer before he leaves for college.

For now, though, he stands on top of the table with a grin, enjoying the fact that all eyes are on him. He ruffles his blond hair, then screams, his voice already a bit hoarse, "It's truth-or-dare time, everyone!"

A mixture of groans and excited squeals fill the room, and I even hear a loud "Yeehaw!" from somewhere in the crowd.

"Basic!" someone else yells.

Blake turns around at that, pointing his cup toward the girl who said it. His face is all serious, and for a second, I really am convinced he's going to throw a tantrum because someone called the classic game boring. But what comes out of his mouth is a simple "Your mom." Then he dramatically drops the red cup he was holding, and before it even hits the floor, people are howling with laughter.

Nina rolls her eyes but immediately drags me to the middle of the room, where people are quickly sitting down in a circle. After a minute or so, it seems like everyone who wants (or, in my case, is being forced) to play is here, so Blake claps his hands once and continues talking.

"Okay, the rules are simple. I spin this bottle, and whoever it points at gets to pick between truth or dare. Either you tell the truth or take a shot, or you do the dare or take a shot." He grins, positioning an empty beer bottle in the middle of our circle. "Now, let's begin."

With that, he lets the bottle decide whose turn it is.

First up is Abigail, a girl from my year who chooses dare and immediately regrets that decision when she's told to reveal her crush by kissing them. A blush colors her cheeks, one that deepens once the crowd starts booing her for reaching for the shot of tequila.

"What a coward. Next!" Blake demands. Everyone laughs, and even though I can see Abigail's hands trembling as she sits back down, I laugh along. Guilt lodges in my throat, but I have to push through it, just like I do every time. I can't afford to think about how it makes her feel, can't afford to realize I was in her place just a few years ago, unless I want to end up back there.

Still, relief fills my chest when everyone moves on.

Another dare follows after that—this time one that's fulfilled. Stephan gets blindfolded and has to kiss two girls. Luckily, he correctly guesses that the second one is Stephanie, his girlfriend. Through the next few rounds, she smiles so brightly that you'd think she won the dating lottery.

More dares keep coming, most of them also involving kissing, of course. Because what else can we possibly do if we're not constantly sticking our tongues in each other's mouths?

No matter how often it happens, though, people cheer every single time, like others kissing because of peer pressure is a movie scene nobody can get enough of. I much prefer watching four seasons of a slow-burn romance show in which the touch of hands makes everyone lose it, but maybe that's just me.

I cheer along.

Eventually, for what feels like the thirteenth time tonight, the bottle spins and spins and spins around again . . . until it doesn't. Gasps and oohs fill the room in an instant, and as I follow everyone's gazes, I find Daniel across the room. He's sitting with his usual friends—Mike and Oliver—who are both laughing because of course they are. The bottle pointing at him is *so hilarious,* top-tier humor *for sure.*

Daniel, however, drinks from his cup, not a single trace of laughter to be seen on his blank face as he looks right at me.

Even from this distance, I know what it means. Not that he wants this to stop or that he's miserable because he already misses me. The truth is far simpler: He's drunk. So. Very. Drunk.

And even though people at school like to say alcohol makes everything and everyone more fun, my ex-boyfriend is the living proof that that's not the case at all. Because, to be completely honest, Drunk Daniel is a total asshole—one who makes impulsive decisions that hurt the people around him.

Suddenly, I think of Susannah, the girl Daniel dated before we became a thing. I remember seeing the two of them sit together in the school cafeteria, hands all over each other while they were surrounded by their mutual friends. The next day, the two of them were broken up, and a week later, Daniel, Mike, and Oliver started sitting with Nina and me. Daniel often referred to his ex as heartless, especially in the first week of sitting at our table, but he never gave much of an explanation for why they broke up. He didn't really need to, though. To this day, the words *Susannah* and *heartless bitch* still get used interchangeably in the hallways.

People believe whatever he says so easily that I can't help but wonder: If Daniel were to say something bad about me, would people believe that without a second thought, too?

I'm frozen. Daniel keeps looking at me until Blake pats him on the back. "It's calling to you, dude. So tell us: Truth or dare?"

*Please choose dare,* I beg him silently.

"Truth," he says instead.

All hope leaves my body, taking the warmth along with it until I'm left cold. I hug myself tighter, bracing myself for the question Blake is obviously going to ask him. There's no way word hasn't gotten around yet. Plus, like I said: These games always cause drama, and though he wouldn't admit it, drama is what Blake lives for. It's one of the reasons he insists on picking truths and dares for everyone.

"Truth, huh?" he says. His usual judgment for when someone picks this option is gone. "Easy. Why don't you tell us why you and your beloved girlfriend Eleanore Young broke up?"

And to make it all worse, the guy actually points at me. As if using my full name didn't make me flinch badly enough already.

*God, I can't wait for him to leave town.*

I force my hands to stay still in my lap, even though I feel like I'll explode if I don't move right this second. I want to do something, want to stim, want an outlet for the nerves that are now coursing through my body, but I can't because of *Rule #6: Keep your hands still when you talk (and, actually, also when you don't). Always be aware of your movements before you accidentally do something that's considered weird.*

I cannot break this. Especially not right now, with so many eyes pointed at me.

A few girls turn to me with sympathetic looks on their faces, but they're definitely in the minority. Most people are glancing between Daniel and me hungrily, waiting for things to blow up.

They're being so unsubtle about it that I wouldn't be surprised if someone pulled out fresh popcorn right this second.

My ex-boyfriend clears his throat. "Well, I broke up with her for a simple reason, but I guess it's important to know a bit about why we started dating in the first place," he tells everyone, looking around like he's giving some sort of presentation. "It's pretty obvious that Ellie isn't an open book despite her being one of the most popular girls in our year. When the two of us started dating, though, I thought that—that maybe I could finally start to understand Willowmoor High's favorite mystery better.

"I mean, as her boyfriend, that couldn't be too hard, right? Since we liked each other and all that stuff. But guess what I discovered?" He pauses, and it's like nobody breathes until he shrugs and says, his words slurring together just a little, "The reason we don't know anything about her is that there's nothing more to Eleanore Young than meets the eye. She's just another cute but boring girl who barely has a personality, and *that* is why we broke up."

After those words, he asks Blake for a refill. Casually. Like my world didn't just go up in flames.

I'll admit my inner monologue is often dramatic, but when I say this is my biggest nightmare, I mean it. It's the thing I've been fearing since . . . forever. The thing younger Ellie would think of while blowing out her birthday candles, wishing it would never happen in the future. Not again.

I still remember how it was in middle school. All I had to

do back then was talk too loudly or smile too wide, and just like that, the other kids would stare at me, whispering or sometimes even shouting about how strange I was. Telling me I wasn't like them. I tried to carry the weight of those words on my shoulders, tried to keep my back straight despite how heavy they got, but they still pushed me down. Down, down, down, trapping me in a spiral of self-loathing. What was wrong with me? Why couldn't I be the kind of person worthy of having friends who weren't my brother?

When high school came around, though, I knew I could change that . . . and myself. I made up my rules and kept to them, and eventually Nina started to show interest in me. Sure, it was probably because she wanted to get closer to my brother, but it started our friendship all the same. Being associated with her good reputation made people slowly forget all about the "weird kid" I was before. Instead, they started to actually like me. Kind, thoughtful, supportive Eleanore Young.

My therapist wasn't happy when I told her about my rules since she thinks it's basically my way of hiding who I really am. She calls it masking and says it's common for autistic people like me to do, but she also says it's not our job to constantly change ourselves to please other people. And she's right. Of course she is. I wouldn't judge someone for being like me, but still. I don't know. If masking is what it takes to be treated like a human being, then I guess it's worth it for me.

With my rules, I thought I had cracked the code. I thought the words *too much* and *not good enough* would never apply to me again, yet here we are. Back to where I started.

“Oh, and also,” Daniel continues after downing his new drink, no emotion whatsoever in his voice. Like he doesn’t realize he’s unraveling me in front of everyone we know. “The two of us dated for six months, but Ellie always avoided going anywhere private with me. Pretty much the only times I’ve been alone with her were so we could kiss.” Suddenly a bitter laugh escapes him. “I mean, that’s not normal behavior, right? I had to break up with her in my car on the way here. All so I wouldn’t be the asshole who broke up with her in public.”

“Bro,” Mike tells him, “that still makes you an asshole.”

Daniel at least has the decency to pause, thinking it over. But all he eventually says is “It’s fine. There are no hard feelings between us. Right, Ellie?”

And then, finally, he looks me in the eyes again. I tense under his cold gaze, swallowing audibly even in this loud room.

“Okay, that’s enough,” Nina says sharply from next to me. She grabs my wrist and starts dragging me out of the circle. With her other hand, she flips off the group. I don’t have the energy to fight her, even though all I can think is *Oh no. Oh no, oh no, oh no.*

There are whispers everywhere in and near the circle. People talk and look and laugh and make up their minds about me until, just like that, everything I ever did to avoid being the weird girl has been erased.

Now all I am is that odd, boring girl, all because Daniel decided so.

I follow my only friend through the sea of people. Nina holds on to me like she’s scared I’ll run away if she lets go, and maybe

I should have, because when we come to a stop, it's in front of the last person I want to ask for help.

Noah is busy talking to two of his friends, so for a split second I am naive enough to believe I can still flee the scene without being noticed. Then his eyes land on me, and he stops in the middle of his sentence. He turns to me, worry and confusion mixed in his frown.

I'm standing too close to him to act like I wasn't going to say something. So, genius that I am, I decide to greet him with a forced smile. "Hi, No," I say, my voice cracking even though only four letters leave my mouth.

At the use of his ancient nickname, Noah goes into full-on protective brother mode, immediately dragging me to the door. He doesn't even apologize to his friends for leaving so abruptly, but he does give Nina a thankful nod I'm sure I'll hear more about soon.

Once we're outside and fresh air fills my lungs, Noah turns to me again, all wide eyes and worry. "What's up, Ellie? Are you okay?"

I look away from his intense gaze. A knot ties itself in my chest, and I know I shouldn't be ashamed to ask for help, especially from Noah. He's my brother *and* one of the kindest people I've ever met, but after so many months of me pushing him away, it feels wrong to expect anything from him.

Still, I ask, "Can you— Could you please take me home?"

Noah blinks a few too many times in surprise before finally recollecting himself. "Yeah, sure," my twin brother tells me, his expression softening. "Let's go home."

## 2. When Nobody's Got You, Remember Your Pros-and-Cons List's Got You

Okay, so . . . I might have lied a little when I said my rules have never failed me. Yes, they've definitely made high school more bearable, but tonight isn't the first time things have blown up in my face. In fact, the last time someone I love found out about the list, I had to lock them out of my life—and my bedroom—completely.

It's the hardest thing I've ever had to do, but every good thing comes with some kind of sacrifice, right?

When Noah was in my room sometime during our first year of high school, he stumbled upon the piece of paper I'd written the first six rules on. People have always liked Noah for who he is—the nice, talkative, laid-back twin—so of course he didn't get it. Said no one's approval is worth changing myself for.

Up until then, Noah and I had been best friends. Not because we were twins and our parents forced us to be, but because he was genuinely, without a doubt, my favorite person in existence. I wanted to keep him close to me for the rest of our lives, but that just wasn't a possibility after that night. Not when Noah made it his personal mission to make me forget my rules.

The breaking point was when he told Nina she could stop pretending to be my friend because he would never go out with her, no matter how hard she tried to get close to him. Nina came to me in tears after that, saying she hoped I knew Noah was not the reason we were friends, that her feelings for my brother were one thing but our friendship was something else entirely. Something she didn't want to lose over a boy.

The next week, Nina had convinced herself to forget all about what Noah had told her, ready to once again commit to the long game of winning his heart. I couldn't shake his words as easily, though. I've always known my best friend's initial interest in me had little to do with who I was and everything to do with my brother, but Noah trying to sabotage our friendship over it still went too far for me.

When I confronted my brother about it, he called Nina selfish and cruel. He said that someone like her would only ever abuse my kindness, never actually like me—the real Ellie, the one only he and our parents knew. That's when I realized the only way to stop him from ruining my chances of becoming likable was by pushing him away. By erasing the version of me he remembered.

So I made up one final rule.

*Rule #7: Don't, under any circumstances, let anyone see the "real" you. Once you let your guard down completely around a person, they'll be able to see right through you—and the last thing you need is for someone to set everything you've been trying to hide free.*

The rest is history.

I never hid that I think it's bullshit when people believe having a twin means you are magically connected and can, for example, finish each other's thoughts, but I do get where the theory comes from. Because having to distance myself from Noah? It really did feel like ripping a piece of my heart out of my own chest.

I've been keeping him at arm's length for almost three years now, which is why, when we get into the car to drive away from this party, he knows better than to ask me what happened. Instead, he puts on some music and lets me stare out the window in peace as I try to think of a way to fix the mess that is my life.

Or, at least, I thought that was what we were doing. But after a minute of total silence, Noah starts talking.

"So," he says, stretching the word out as if I haven't had enough awkward car rides today. "Speaking of our last year of high school . . ."

I keep my head turned away from him, looking at the dark night sky so he can't see the way my lips twitch in an attempt not to laugh at the absurdity of his comment. It's just so typically Noah.

"I was thinking about how that means this will probably be the last year we ever really live together, too." I look at him, and he smiles sadly. A few seconds of silence pass between us before he says, "I know you're only coming to SMASH! to spend more time with Daniel, but maybe we could hang out a bit while we're there, too? We haven't been close for a few years now, but I . . . I miss you, Ellie. A lot. And I really don't want the distance between us to become impossible to cross when we both move away for college."

I push the first half of what he said as far away from me as I can. "Our colleges are likely going to be hundreds of miles away from each other, Noah. There's little we can do to change that." I clear my throat. "But that fact aside, Daniel and I just broke up, actually. So I guess I'll have a whole lot of time to spend with you at camp. If you truly want that."

Noah scans my face for something, but judging by his frown, he doesn't find what he's looking for. "I'm really . . . *sorry* to hear about you and Daniel," he says, careful, even though I know for a fact he never liked my ex-boyfriend. He swallows. "But for the record, I wasn't talking about the literal distance. I'm just scared that if we keep walking past each other like we've been doing for the past few years, we will lose touch completely—until one day we're two estranged forty-year-olds who have way too many regrets and no way to repair their broken relationship!"

Even as the words tumble out of his mouth, he tries to keep his tone lighthearted, adding a nervous laugh at the end. But I know Noah, and he only rambles like this when he feels helpless.

I press my lips together tightly, the words I want to ignore now echoing through my head. *I miss you, Ellie.* It'd be so easy for me to confess that I miss him, too, to let him back into my life just a little bit. I'm allowed to have this one real thing, right?

But I wouldn't even know how to let him in, so I let my gaze drop to my hands instead, which earns me a deep sigh from Noah.

"Come on, Ellie," he says softly, his voice breaking a little. "You know you can't keep doing this for the rest of your life, right? And what better time to forget about your list than right now? It's like in those books you're always reading!" he pushes. "It's summer, you're about to be at camp, away from home and outside your comfort zone, and deep down you know it's time for a change. A big one. My job as the side character is to convince you to actually take that chance!"

I stare at him, blinking. "Wait, you read my romance novels? And why are you acting like they're all the same?"

A grin tugs at his mouth. "First of all, there *definitely* is a pattern most of them follow, and you know how much I love analyzing stuff like that. So yeah, I might've stolen—I mean *borrowed* a few, but we both know that's beside the point I'm trying to make right now. Please just think about it, Ellie. Okay?"

And I do. Even though I'm trying so hard not to think about what he's saying, I do. Because of course he's right, and suddenly memories of everything he's ever said about beach volleyball camp return to me. He started going the summer after I shut him out, so I only know stuff from conversations he had at the dinner table with our parents, but what I've heard from him is exactly what I need. I can recall multiple conversations in which Noah rambled on and on about how summer camp is where he can be the truest version of himself. Where he can show parts of who he is that he didn't even know existed.

And wouldn't that solve all my problems?

One summer with people I'll never have to see again. A summer for learning to let go, for messing up as much as I want without being judged . . . and for trying to become fun enough so that, at the end of all this, Daniel will want me back, thus proving to everyone at school that what he said about me isn't true.

It's the perfect solution.

When we get home, I run to my room and open up my favorite notebook. I write and write and write, my hands shaking a little with excitement as I do so. Partly because making pros-and-cons lists makes me embarrassingly happy, but also because this could work. I could actually fix all this.

Once I drop my pen next to me, I don't even have to reread the pros and cons I wrote down in order to know what I'm going to do.

In a few weeks, I'll be at beach volleyball camp, studying the people around me and learning how to be more like myself again. More fun. All I need is to complete this simple checklist:

- ☐ *Allow yourself to talk more.*
- ☐ *Don't overthink too much.*
- ☐ *Stop holding back your laughter.*
- ☐ *Learn how to get vulnerable again.*
- ☐ *Let yourself fall in love.*

Bye, rumors. Bye, whispers. Bye, staring. Just like that, my senior year of high school will be saved.

# 3. Don't Make Impulsive Decisions (. . . This Might Be a Bit Too Late)

To absolutely no one's surprise, actions have consequences, and on August first, I have to deal with a whole list of them.

For starters, I've barely gotten any sleep. Thanks to my annoying little brain full of its annoying little thoughts, I lay awake for most of the night, tossing and turning and unable to relax a single muscle in my body. With the amount of stressing I did, you'd think I was being sent to my death today rather than some silly summer camp named SMASH! Though I suppose that, if you look at it poetically, I *am* dying today—the old me is, at least.

Luckily, I'm not a poet.

Another consequence I'm not too happy with is the fact that the drive from Willowmoor to Bloomdale will take an hour and a half. That means that for the next—I glance at the GPS—hour and twenty-five minutes, I'll be stuck in this car, trying not to groan whenever I get stress-induced cramps.

I sink a little in my seat and put one hand over my stomach, using the other to pointlessly scroll through my phone. Somehow, without thinking about it, my fingers open my chat with Daniel. It looks the same as it has for three weeks now, his four text messages from the morning after the party still unanswered.

**DANIEL:**

hey

i am so sorry about last night

it's honestly all a blur to me now

but i really did mean it when i said there should be no hard feelings between us

so i'm sorry if drunk me ruined that

I want to tell him it's okay, want to reply that I get it and that I forgive him. We could move on to our next chapter—the one in which I win him back and we fall hopelessly in love—but I can't. Not yet. Because for the time being, my forgiveness would be a lie.

So, I still haven't replied.

Before I close the chat, I reread Daniel's messages one more time. I know his words by heart at this point, but seeing them on my screen still makes me want to throw my phone out the window. Or, even better, my whole existence. Instead my hands tighten around my phone until my knuckles are white, as if I'm hoping I can squeeze every bit of life out of it.

"You okay?" Noah asks from next to me, a slight crease between his eyebrows when I turn his way and drop my phone.

"It's nothing I'm not used to. I get my period every month, you know," I lie. In reality, I was on my period last week, but Noah doesn't know that, so it's an easy excuse. Since I really don't feel like admitting the thought of summer camp is making me physically ill, I straighten my back a bit, trying to give him a forced smile through another uncomfortable shot of pain.

My brother takes a sip of water, his short brown hair already clinging to his forehead from sweat. Dad's black car is an oven at this point, despite the air-conditioning working its ass off to make the temperature more bearable, and with the sun still out, it's not bound to get better anytime soon. Florida summers are *brutal*.

Noah puts his water bottle back in the cooler, then turns to me. "It's going to be fun, Ellie. Just . . . trust me."

I know I'm not the best liar, but seriously? How did he see through my lie that quickly?

I thought I'd feel prepared for this. I really, really did, but even though the last consequence on this mental list of mine was inevitable the moment I promised Daniel I would come along months ago, it's somehow still the thing that has caught me off guard the most. Because right now, I'm actually on my way to *beach volleyball summer camp*.

"Noah is right, sweetie," Mom chimes in, turning to look at me with a smile from the passenger seat. "We realize how big and scary new things like this are for you, but stepping out of your comfort zone is going to pay off." Her lips part again as she hesitates before saying, "You know, you were such a happy child before middle school—always laughing as loud as you wanted and talking everyone's ears off." Her smile falters. "It's been so sad to see you lose that light you used to always carry. I really think SMASH! is exactly what you need. A place to be yourself with people who will show you how much that is worth." She swallows, her eyes glazed over with emotion. "I hope you can find your sunshine again, my love."

I look away, having to break our eye contact as the ache in my heart becomes too much to face her. "I hope so, too."

When I took some distance from my parents, I thought I was just protecting them. During my time in middle school, when I was being bullied, they had to deal with so much. Calls with the school, appointments with my therapist, and that's not even including my almost-daily mental breakdowns. Mom always told me how much it broke her heart to see me like that, so I . . . I thought that by locking everything up inside me, I'd spare her some hurt. That as long as I pretended to be fine, she wouldn't have to worry about me at all. But I never considered how it must've been for her and Dad to see how their daughter locked herself away.

Maybe Daniel isn't the only reason I should let go of my rules. Maybe it's about time I do this.

Mom reaches for my hand, and when I give it to her, she squeezes. "We're so proud of you, Eleanore."

Dad hums in agreement from behind the steering wheel, glancing at Mom for a second before turning away, only to then look back at her again. "Are you really crying over our daughter going to a camp named SMASH!, Carolyn?" he teases.

"Finally!" I exclaim, glad to see the conversation take a turn that doesn't make the air around me feel so heavy. "I've been waiting for someone to address the name!"

Mom shakes her head, quickly wiping away the little tear that was starting to leave her eye. "I think it's a fun name! And I'm not *crying*. My eyes are just . . . sweating a little."

"With this heat, I honestly could believe that," Noah says, sweeping some of the sweat off his forehead once again.

I reach for my bottle of water, somehow resisting the urge to pour it all over me so I can cool down a bit more, even if just for a moment. After a good sip of water, I take another look at the clock. An hour and twenty minutes left in this car slash oven.

Surely I will survive.

Given the fact that I've decided to join a beach volleyball camp, you'd think I wouldn't mind a little sand between my toes, but let's get one thing straight right now: I very much do.

I've barely set foot on the beach when a shiver goes through me. This sensation should be such a small, barely noticeable thing, but there's something about the way the tiny grains of sand scrape against each other that I feel in every single part of my body. It travels from my toes to my belly and from my shoulders all the way to my brain, scratching it in the most unpleasant of ways.

And I have a whole two weeks of this feeling to look forward to. *Just . . . great.*

I consider turning back around and running after Mom and Dad's car in hopes of them taking me home with them, but I know Noah wouldn't let me. And besides, I don't think I'm physically capable of running that fast, but oh well. A girl can dream.

My brother is to my left, his feet strolling through the sand as he is seemingly unbothered by one of the worst feelings in the world. "Are you ready for your life-changing summer, Ellie?"

I lift my gaze from our feet to his eyes. In this light, his irises are a brighter blue than usual, the gray in the blue-gray eye color we share becoming less evident with the sun shining on our faces. It's not the same shade as that of the sky above us or the ocean that's approaching, but it's still blue. As I take in both him and our surroundings, it's impossible not to feel like he belongs here.

Even though we look alike, I can't imagine the same is true for me.

Still, I say truthfully, "As ready as I'll ever be."

We near a crackling campfire surrounded by dozens of teenagers, and I can already hear some of the chatter and laughter from here. It feels very peaceful, and as I take a deep breath and let the evening air fill my lungs, my heart rate starts to slow down.

Until it picks up again when someone lets out a ridiculously loud scream.

"IT'S NOAH! OH MY GOD!" the person yells, and just like that, all heads whip in our direction.

For a second, everything is completely silent, and the next, a group of screaming people are running across the beach so they can throw themselves into my brother's arms. They're so fast that I can barely even catch a glance of their faces, and I doubt they've noticed my existence at all.

As I stand there, a few inches away from the group, I turn to one of the people who came along with them but hasn't joined in on the hug, either. She's Black and is wearing a deep red hijab. When she notices that I've noticed her, she gives me a knowing smile.

"First year, too?" she asks, at which I nod. "Nice to meet you. I'm Yasmeen, she/her."

No one has ever introduced themselves to me with their pronouns before—almost everyone at school thinks it's weird or unnecessary to do so—but something about it instantly warms my heart. "Ellie," I tell her, the corners of my mouth lifting automatically. "My pronouns are she/her as well."

Before the two of us get to say anything else, Noah breaks free of his friends with a laugh and walks back to me. He turns to the group. "Everyone, meet Ellie. My sister," he tells them.

"Welcome to SMASH!" A white girl with short, dark red–dyed hair and a nose ring smiles up at me.

"This is Max," Noah lets me know, but a second later Max is already gone, screaming and running away to hug another new arrival. "Well, that *was* Max," Noah says now. Four other people rush after her as soon as they've welcomed me, telling me their names so quickly that I can't process a single one.

When they're gone, Noah and his friends walk back to a spot near the campfire where a gap was created. My brother sits down next to the tallest of the group, and the person sitting next to Yasmeen leaves some room between themself and Noah so I can settle there. It's thoughtful, and I really do appreciate it, but I would honestly rather keep standing for the rest of eternity than sit down in this circle.

Still, after a few more seconds of pitying myself, I sit down, trying not to cringe as my butt meets the sand. I quite obviously fail.

"These two are my best friends, by the way," Noah informs me, managing to distract me from my struggle. "Liam and Maya."

"Hi!" the short one greets me, a big grin on their face. "I'm Maya, they/them." They have brown skin and short black hair that only just covers their ears. They keep having to readjust their bangs because of the wind. "It's so nice to finally meet you."

Then I move my eyes to the other person. The tall one. "That makes me Liam. He/they pronouns. This guy right here has told us a lot about you," he lets me know, patting my brother on the back. Both Noah and I look down, cheeks red, but when I lift my gaze to meet Liam's again, he's smiling warmly, no bite to it. He doesn't seem to want me to feel like an intruder, and all I can think is *Wow, people here already are different from my classmates at school.*

Or maybe I'm just not reading them correctly. This wouldn't be the first time that happened, actually.

My brother turns to Yasmeen next. "And this is . . ." He trails off, not knowing what to say about my fellow newcomer.

"Yasmeen," she helps him with a laugh. "I'm Maya's girlfriend."

The word *girlfriend* rolls off her tongue so easily, and without overthinking it, she grabs Maya's hand. My heart grows in size until it feels like it's trying to escape the cage that is my chest, but I will it to stay calm.

*Don't be weird about this.*

It's just that I absolutely *love* love, and though I devour a romance book every other week, it's pretty rare for me to see people my age be this unmistakably in love with each other in real life. Even with Daniel and me, it wasn't that way. Sure, we kissed pretty much daily, and occasionally we had our romance novel–worthy moments, like when he walked me home in the rain. But we weren't in love.

Not yet, at least.

Maybe if I succeed at winning him back, though, we can be more like Maya and Yasmeen. We could form a deeper connection instead of just tolerating each other again.

Maybe then I could find the love I've always been scared isn't in the cards for me.

Noah's jaw has dropped open in response to Yasmeen and Maya, resulting in the rest of the group laughing. For a second, I want to force myself to laugh along with them so I fit in, but then I realize I don't have to follow those rules anymore.

*Just try to be yourself, Eleanore,* I remind myself. But instead of actually having the guts to join in on the conversation, I simply continue watching them.

"Maya, you asshole!" Noah says to his friend, pushing at their shoulder playfully. "I can't believe you kept this from me! You literally sent a meme about the useless lesbian stereotype to the group chat just yesterday, and I said you were only useless when it came to flirting . . ."

That only makes Maya laugh louder. They wrap their arm around their girlfriend, pulling her close until they're sitting hip to hip. "That really was hilarious, though. I just didn't want to miss the expression on your face once you found out! Nothing is more fun than seeing your soul leave your body for a moment."

"Oh! Speaking of dying on the spot, Noah," Liam starts a little too excitedly, which earns him a glare from my brother. "I've got some news for you as well. According to some sources, Sloane is joining us at camp again this year."

Noah's entire body tenses, and I watch as another blush creeps onto his face.

I see a chance for me to join in on the conversation, and this time, I'm too nosy not to grab it. "Who is Sloane?" I ask, my voice a bit shakier than I want it to be, like I've somehow forgotten how to use it already.

Maya pats Noah on his back. "You have a few seconds to recover while I catch your sister up on our lore, dude," they tell him, then turn back to me. "Sloane was a camper two years ago, and our dear Noah developed a massive, *pathetic* crush on her, but before he found the courage to make a move, she disappeared. The poor guy never got over it."

"But," Liam starts, "things could change this year with her return."

Noah considers this for a second, then shakes his head, clearly trying not to get hopeful about this. "Oh please. Where did you even get this information?"

"Julia told me."

My brother snorts. "A very reliable source, I'm sure, but if *we* couldn't find Sloane on social media last year, I doubt she magically messaged Julia, of all people, that she's coming back."

Liam shrugs. "Julia is a really good stalker, though. Much better than us, but I guess we'll just have to wait and—"

Before he gets the chance to finish that sentence, one of the people sitting around the campfire suddenly stands up to shout, "SMASH! SMASH! SMASH!" They repeatedly pump their fist in the air as they do so, and I've barely processed what exactly it is they're doing when someone else joins in . . . and then another person . . . and a dozen others, too. Until almost everyone, including my own brother, is screaming the camp's name.

Yasmeen and I share a look. "Have we stumbled into a cult?" she asks me. She has to yell in order for me to hear.

I assume she doesn't expect me to actually answer her question.

After a minute or so, the chants of SMASH! turn into whoops as a man in his fifties gets on his feet. "Patience, please. We're still waiting for a few more minutes," he tells the enthusiastic crowd seriously. Noah quickly informs me that this is the guy who owns the camp, and I can't help but frown.

He seems awfully grumpy for someone who decided to name his summer camp SMASH!

A minute passes. Then a blond twentysomething woman wearing a camp counselor T-shirt appears from behind a corner, followed by a girl with two braids in her auburn hair. The girl's eyes are pointed at the sand beneath her.

Before I have the time to fully take her in, my brother makes a noise. "Oh," he supposedly says, but it sounds more like he just choked on his own spit.

I glance at Noah—or rather, at what's left of "the poor guy," as

Maya put it. Liam is looking, too, letting out a sigh and shaking his head at the sight of his best friend. "Just as I predicted." And, well, he does really look like he just died a thousand deaths, so I don't even bother asking if this is indeed Sloane.

The girl walks until she's a part of the crowd, but she doesn't join any of the small groups, instead standing alone as the camp's owner clears his throat.

"Well then," he says once people have returned their attention to him, "I guess it's time we start with the initiation. Gigi?"

I turn to Noah. "I'm sorry, the *what* now?"

My brother makes a face. "I can't tell you, but you'll find out soon enough," he says, taking his eyes off Sloane for just a second to give me a reassuring smile. "It's nothing extreme, though. Don't worry about it."

"I'm, in fact, worrying about it," I whisper back, my eyes wide, but he's already moved on to trying to catch Sloane's attention. She continues to look at the ground.

The blond camp counselor—Gigi—runs up to the owner until they're side by side, him with his lips pressed together tightly and her beaming as she scans the crowd. She puts her big sunglasses on top of her head. "Welcome to SMASH!, everyone!" she yells, which is answered by screaming that's so loud, you'd almost think we're at a concert and the artist just entered the stage.

Except I've never been to a concert, so I wouldn't actually know if that's accurate.

"We know you're all eager to catch up with old friends or get to know everyone who you don't already know, so I think it's best if we kick off this camp with a little game." Gigi grins. "The rules are simple. First, grab a few pieces of paper from this bucket. Then walk around the campfire until you bump into someone, which is when you'll open up one of your pieces of paper and wordlessly make your new friend guess what's written on it. If you both guess correctly, then you can briefly introduce yourselves to each other."

"Wait, isn't that just charades?" I hear what I guess is a fifteen-year-old girl whisper to her friend. And she's right, of course, which is just *such* great news for me. After all, I'm *exceptional* at catching neurotypical people's hints.

Gigi hands the bucket to one of the campers sitting close to her. "Let's start!"

Just like that, more people grab pieces of paper from the bucket. In a matter of seconds, some campers are already walking around or even frantically shouting things in an attempt to guess their partner's word.

Noah gets off the ground beside me as well, after which he offers me his hand. I gladly take it, following him to the bucket to grab some words for myself. I've barely been able to look at my word—*dream*—when Noah starts acting something out.

He flaps his arms around him really fast, like they're wings, and it's so simple, even I can't misunderstand it. "You're a really strange bird?" I ask, trying not to laugh at the sight of him.

He shoots me a look but does bring his arms back to his sides.

Now it's my turn, so I make a fake pillow out of my hands and let my head rest on them, closing my eyes.

"Sleep!" Noah guesses immediately, which is fair, but I shake my head. I settle back into my position, and this time, I let out a wistful sigh, almost like I'm longing for something. "Dreaming!" he exclaims now, and I open my eyes back up.

Surely the verb counts, too.

My brother offers me his hand again, this time to shake it. "Hi, stranger," he says, dimples forming in his cheeks as I hold his gaze. "We make quite a good team. My name is Noah, by the way."

"Eleanore," I tell him. The smile on my face must be identical to his, except for the fact that I have only one dimple, in my left cheek. "But you can call me Ellie."

Next, I try to guess a fellow brown-haired girl's word while also attempting to find a way to act out the word *trash*. I fail, and thus she disappears without telling me her name. Afterward, I bump into a person with a blue buzz cut. They guessed the word *ladder* correctly, which I'll take as a win, thank you very much, but I'll never know what they were trying to show me. So, still no name.

The next word I get is *French fries*, and honestly, that's when I start to doubt that being autistic is the only reason I'm having such a hard time with this. Like, how can literally anyone act out the words *French fries*? The boy in front of me miraculously guesses the *fries* part, but when I try to make him add *French* in front of it by signifying a baguette, I lose him.

At the end of the game, I don't know a single person's name.

"All right, everyone," the camp's owner says. "You can return to the circle. Before we tell you who your teammate is and what cabin you're in, though, we've got to go over some rules."

While everyone settles back down, I let my gaze wander. Whether they're fourteen, fifteen, or nearing seventeen like me, everywhere I look, there are people whose names I don't know and whose stories I haven't heard. A place full of strangers. All new faces with no memories attached to them. Hope fills my chest as I think about the endless possibilities lying ahead of me.

*This is going to be* my *summer,* I tell myself.

But as soon as the thought enters my mind, I spot the one and only Daniel Solomon. And he sees me, too.

For the first time since I've known him, the entire world around us seems to fade away. There's no constant chatter in the background, no nosy teenagers who can see our every move, no heart beating out of my chest. It's just me and Daniel . . . and my nausea.

Is this really the feeling people search for all their lives? Because if so, I would gladly hand it over.

Seconds pass as we hold each other's gaze, but after a bit, he does look away, immediately returning his attention to his group of camp friends. Like he doesn't know who I am at all.

I have no choice but to try to do the same. Going up to him so soon will make me seem desperate, which is the last thing I need Daniel to think.

No, I need to regain his interest first. Guys like him love the chase, so it's best if I let him come to me.

I scan the people around me who are already sitting down.

My eyes fall onto the semifamiliar face of Lily, a member of Willowmoor High's volleyball team. A few feet away from her sits a girl who is laughing at something her friend said, and even though we've never properly interacted before, I recognize her as Vera, who is in the year below me at Willowmoor High.

I try to see if I know anyone else, but most faces don't spark any memories. That is, until I spot a girl I share some of my classes with, though I don't think we've ever exchanged more than two words, both being *hello*.

"That's Sierra, right?" I ask Noah, my eyes still on her. She's standing all by herself, blond hair up in the same ponytail she always wears to school, and her eyes don't seem to be searching for anyone, either. "I've seen her around at school. Is this her first year here?"

Maya overhears and shakes their head. "She's been coming here for longer than any of us, but she doesn't really have any friends at camp."

I take Sierra in once again. "Then why does she keep coming back?" I ask.

"Oh, she doesn't *want* to make any friends, honey. Feels like she's too good for any of us, I guess, since her dad is Adrian Levine," Liam explains. He waits for realization to dawn on my face, but when I don't react, he continues. "You know, *the* beach volleyball legend of Florida? Adrian Levine? Dude, have you really never heard of . . . ?"

I can't help myself. I laugh at the ridiculousness of my being here. Seriously, why did I *ever* agree to come along with Daniel?

*Because that's what good girlfriends are supposed to do,* I remind myself.

I clear my throat. "It's a long story, but I actually know close to nothing about beach volleyball," I admit to Liam.

He opens his mouth, then closes it again. "Okay, that's fine, I guess, but you're literally standing four steps away from him." They point at the camp's owner and inform me, "*That* is Adrian Levine."

And it is at this very moment that I realize I am truly unprepared for this summer.

An ashamed blush colors my cheeks, but before Liam gets to say anything about that, the camp's owner—Adrian, aka Sierra's dad—whistles. Loudly.

My hands fly to my ears, as if I can protect them from the noise that's already gone.

"Okay, everyone!" Adrian says when most people have paused their conversations. He's loud enough that the eighty people at camp can hear him. Unlike with Gigi, there's no real enthusiasm in his voice. "It's time to go over some rules!"

Just like that, he starts telling us what we should do and, most importantly, what we absolutely should *not* do. No food or sodas in the cabins where we will be sleeping. Water is fine, of course. If we damage any property, we'll have to pay for repairs. A single drop of alcohol will get us sent home immediately. Also, he doesn't really care when we go to sleep but asks us to please not keep others up by being loud.

The list goes on and on and on, but everything on it seems reasonable and fine.

After going over it all, Adrian takes a deep breath. "Basically, it all comes down to this one rule: Behave yourselves, please. Are there any questions I wasn't able to answer with that?" he asks, and immediately, a hand goes up in the air. "Yes," he says, "you, in the purple shirt?"

"How many people will we be sharing our cabins with? And, oh my god, are there going to be bunk beds?" asks a girl excitedly. I'd guess her to be just fourteen years old.

"Most of you will be in a cabin with four people total, two bunk beds per room." A new hand goes up in the air, at which point Adrian closes his eyes and pinches the bridge of his nose, like he's just given up on his very last bit of faith in humanity. "No, Ashley," he says before even hearing her out, "we can't let you share a room with campers of the opposite sex. Please don't make me explain why."

Her hand goes back down. There's a grin on her face as she whispers something to her friends.

"Heteronormative much," another person tells Adrian, earning some laughs from the group. I turn to where the sound came from, finding Sierra on the opposite side of the campfire. Her face is all serious, seeming to glitch a little thanks to the flames that separate us.

Adrian's eyes flick to his daughter. "Levine," he starts, with a tone that makes it sound like that isn't his last name, too. "Don't make me put you in a solo room."

She simply shrugs. "Go ahead. We both know I wouldn't mind limiting my social interactions."

"You're right, my bad." He thinks it over for a few seconds, slowly nodding to himself. Then he says, "Well, don't make me room you with the kindergartners next door, then."

Her eyes widen. "No way. That's a whole new low, even for you."

All around us, people are whispering to each other, some looking absolutely shocked someone would talk to the camp's owner or their own parent this way. But there's a small spark in Adrian's eyes now, something I didn't expect to see since even the campfire didn't light up his face. For a moment, I'd swear he's close to smiling—which would be a first for today—but then he turns back to the rest of the impatient teenagers surrounding him. He clears his throat.

"Any other questions?" Adrian looks around the group and waits a few more beats to see if anyone else will raise their hand. "Great," he says when no one does. "That means it's time to introduce you to your camp counselors." He quickly tells us who everyone is, from the middle-aged man named David to the twenty-year-old girl who goes by Sam. "Now, Gigi here is going to tell you who your teammates are," he finishes.

Gigi immediately jumps to her feet, not wasting another second. She starts shouting names, which makes people high-five each other or run across the circle to be at their new teammate's side. Others look around the group, waiting to see whose face belongs to the name of their partner.

"Vera Kuang and Naomi Schulz! Maxine Miller and Sujin Choi! Veronica Owens and Sloane Finley!" Gigi continues to shout.

From the corner of my eye, I see Liam freeze. "What's wrong?" Noah asks before I gather the confidence.

Liam shakes their head. "Probably nothing," they say, but their voice trembles with uncertainty. "There's a Veronica Owens at my school who is not exactly known for being, um . . . *kind.* Even her former friends—who literally *outed* people—think she's mean, which is saying quite a lot." He sighs. "Being the awkward Japanese guy at school is already bad enough. I can't have people in my hometown finding out about my pronouns and coming up with even more reasons to bully me. I mean, it would overwhelm their bigoted little brains!"

Liam starts to laugh, but he's the only one. The rest of us just stare at him in worry.

He stops to clear his throat when he notices. "Sorry," he says. "Humor is my coping mechanism, but I forgot I'm not funny. Either way, surely there are thousands of white people named Veronica Owens, so everything is *fine.*"

I want to tell them they can always talk to me about this if they want to, that maybe I will understand some parts of it, though of course not everything, but when I open my mouth, they lift their hand to stop me.

"Nope," he says, grinning. "Our official trauma dump is scheduled for week two, thank you very much."

I mentally make a note to prepare myself for that.

"Maya Shaan and Yasmeen Qadir!" Gigi yells then, and for some reason, that prompts Liam and Noah to congratulate Maya, who is bowing like they just got handed some prestigious award. Their grin is so big, I can almost feel my jaw ache just looking at it.

When I turn to Yasmeen in confusion, she's already waiting

for me to catch her gaze. "Cult," she mouths again, but when her partner asks what she said, she smiles and shakes her head innocently. "Nothing you need to worry about, babe. Why are we celebrating, though? Didn't we choose these teams last month?"

"Right, well, about that," Maya starts, their grin fading into something a bit more cautious. "I knew you wouldn't come along this summer if I told you we don't exactly choose our own teams, so I kind of sort of lied and gave you a fake form?"

Yasmeen murmurs something in a language I don't understand. All I know is it doesn't sound very positive, considering her tone.

"But!" Maya tries. "I was pretty sure we were going to be teammates anyway since we're compatible. The camp counselors make teams by observing us while we play charades and trying to predict who will work well together, so basically: Our relationship is now SMASH! approved."

Yasmeen blankly stares at them for a few seconds, then shakes her head. Still, she can't hide her small smile and the hearts in her eyes when she says, "You're ridiculous. You lied to me!"

I turn to Noah, my stomach dropping as I repeat Maya's words in my head. "Wait, so that's what you couldn't tell me? That we were pretty much being match-made?"

Noah nods. "It's a tradition not to give away that secret to first-years, so I couldn't tell you. I know you don't like surprises, though. I'm sorry, Ellie."

"It's fine," I tell him with a shrug, but I can't shake a feeling of dread as Gigi continues to scream pairs. While we were playing the game, I was so focused on wanting people to guess my words that I barely took the time to talk to anyone except Noah. I didn't connect with anyone else—didn't even *try* to, too caught up in my desperation to be good at the game—and since there don't seem to be any boy-and-girl teams, I doubt I'll end up being paired with my brother.

So who can they team me up with, then? Someone random who doesn't fit anywhere else, either?

I assumed they would make teams based on skill level, especially given the fact that Adrian the-beach-volleyball-legend Levine owns the camp. He doesn't exactly seem like the type for this whole emotional matchmaking stuff, but maybe I'm too quick to judge. After all, he didn't even make us play any volleyball before assigning teams, which is . . . a choice.

"Noah Young and Liam Miyasaki!" Gigi yells then, making my heart stop. "And, lastly, Eleanore Young and Sierra Levine!"

Gigi laughs, saying something about eighty names being a lot to call out, but I only vaguely register the words that are coming out of her mouth at this point, because the only thing I can focus on right now is Sierra. Sierra Levine, the daughter of a retired beach volleyball legend. Sierra, a girl in my class who I somehow have not really talked to before. Sierra, my teammate for the next two weeks who is currently frowning at me from across the crackling campfire.

Well, this is going to be an eventful summer.

# 4. Make a Lasting First Impression—Preferably a Good One

The first thing I notice upon entering one of the dozens of cabins standing next to each other is that it's small. Even without the presence of any closets or desks, there's not much room to freely move around. All the space is taken up by two bunk beds that are almost touching. Aside from that, there's a little window and a door that leads to what I assume is an even smaller bathroom.

It's not a lot, to the point where looking at it makes me feel at least a little claustrophobic, but considering the stories I've heard from Noah over the years, I don't think we'll have much spare time to spend in here. If we're not playing volleyball in the coming weeks, we'll be participating in group activities.

Sierra gets to our cabin not even a minute after me, holding her luggage in her hands. I drop mine in a corner of the room and turn to my brand-new teammate.

"So," I start, scrambling for an icebreaker. What do

neurotypical people like to talk about? Eventually I settle for "The weather is going to be pretty nice this week."

Sierra takes her backpack off her shoulders, letting it slide to the floor. Her dark brown eyes scan my face, and for a moment I think she's looking for a way to keep this conversation from dying too quickly, but in the end all she says is "Yeah." Then she unzips her backpack, eyes no longer on me.

*Well, there goes that topic of conversation.*

"I don't think we've ever really talked before," I continue, knowing it might come across as a bit pushy. Still, I can't help it. Something inside me desperately wants her to like me, for the corners of her mouth to curl up into a smile, even if it's just a polite one. "I go to Willowmoor High, too, though, and you probably do know my brother, Noah."

She nods but doesn't look back up at me. "Yeah, I do. And I know who you are, too, don't worry."

I don't know if that's actually meant to be reassuring, but it sure isn't working.

"Wait," a soft voice behind us suddenly says. It's so quiet and hesitant that I think I must've imagined it, especially since I wasn't aware there was another person here, but when I turn around, I find the girl with two auburn braids standing in the doorway to the bathroom. Sloane.

The third member of cabin 4, apparently.

"You're Noah's sister?" Sloane asks. She closes the bathroom door behind her, and when I nod, she smiles at me. "He, um, told me about you before. A while ago, that is. Your name is Ellie, right? I'm Sloane. One of Noah's . . . friends."

"I know," I say like a total fool.

*Okay,* so maybe I don't need to break all my rules after all. Thinking things over before saying anything might actually prove to be useful.

"Noah mentioned that he was really hoping you'd be back this year," I explain, returning a smile. She breaks our eye contact, looking down at her feet as her cheeks almost instantly color a bright shade of red. *Great job, Eleanore.* "That was a weird thing for me to say, wasn't it? I'm so sorry for making this—"

"No! No! You're completely fine!" she reassures me, but even more heat is rising to her cheeks. "I was just kind of scared to come back because I thought things would be awkward with him. And Liam and Maya," she adds quickly. "I guess it's nice to know they don't completely hate me for disappearing."

I think she's about to say something else, maybe even explain why exactly she disappeared, but before any more words tumble out of her mouth, an unfamiliar voice speaks up.

"Not to interrupt this incredibly awkward conversation," the girl says, "but can we please introduce ourselves? Because I, for one, have no idea what the fuck is going on."

A silence falls over the three of us for a second as we look at the fourth and final member of our cabin. There couldn't be a bigger contrast between sweet, shy Sloane and this new girl, yet the only explanation for her being here is that she's Veronica, the girl who might be from Liam's school and, more importantly, Sloane's teammate.

I take it Sierra and I aren't the only questionable match, then.

Where Veronica's eyes are a piercing kind of green, Sloane's are a calming shade of brown you can't help but immediately feel relaxed around. Her braided auburn hair has a certain warmth to it, while Veronica has short, pitch-black hair that reminds me of a starless night. Her pale white face is all sharp edges, while Sloane still has a soft, embarrassed blush on her cheeks, and where Veronica is wearing all black, Sloane is dressed up in pastel blues.

"Alright." Veronica sighs when no one else dares to break the silence. "I'll go first, then. My name is Veronica, she/her, I live in Grovington, and I'm sixteen years old. I play the drums and indoor volleyball, but I really wanted to give beach volleyball a try, so now I'm here." She nods her head toward Sierra. "Your turn."

Sierra tightens her blond ponytail before saying, "Sure. I'm Sierra, she/her, sixteen years old as well, and I live in Willowmoor. I've been playing both beach and indoor volleyball since I was little. Outside that, I . . ." She pauses for a second before shaking her head and clearing her throat. "I guess that's about it, actually." Then she brings her gaze to meet mine. "What about you, Eleanore?" she asks, her expression still neutral.

I know very little about Sierra Levine. Before last year, when the rumors started spreading around school, I only vaguely knew who she was. To me, she was that one girl who didn't shy away from harsh truths, the one who always called people out on their bullshit, albeit not very kindly. I didn't know her name back then, but I know that I'd wished I had some of her bravery. To most other people at Willowmoor High, however, this didn't make her admirable. It made her a stuck-up bitch.

I only learned her name when it got out that she's gay.

Nobody gave her a hard time about it to her face as far as I know—they were probably too scared to be rightfully called out on their homophobia—but that fear wasn't enough to actually stop them from being homophobic. There were still lots of looks, whispers, and people who said they always knew there was something "off" about her.

And the only thing I did was bite my tongue. No wonder she's looking at me like it wouldn't bother her if a ball hit me in the face. She has every right to feel that way.

*There goes my chance to befriend my teammate,* I think, but then I remember what Liam and Maya said about Sierra—that she's not here to make friends in the first place—and I feel a little bit better. It's comforting, in a way. To know that I can't mess anything up with Sierra because she genuinely couldn't care less about what I do or say.

Still, the thought stings.

I swallow. "I'm Eleanore, she/her, but I go by Ellie," I start. "Right now I'm sixteen years old, and I live in Willowmoor, just like Sierra." I look at her and smile, despite knowing she won't return it. And just like that, it's time to tell them who I really am—who I want to be—besides the basics of my name and age and hometown.

*Alright, Eleanore, just be yourself. And be cool, too. No overthinking allowed.*

"I spend a lot of my free time journaling or reading," I continue. "I also love listening to music a lot while doing that, and . . ." I trail off, not knowing how to finish the sentence.

Why did I even say *and*? There's no *and*!

Still, to try and make it less awkward, I finish by saying the first thing about me that comes to mind. Which ends up with me exclaiming that "I'm autistic? Um, yeah, I just thought you should all know that."

*Well, that's certainly a way to open up to people . . .*

I look at my hands for a good few seconds before daring to make eye contact again. Sloane is giving me a soft, reassuring smile, while Sierra and Veronica nod to themselves, taking in this information. They don't stare at me with open mouths, and there's no dirty or pitying glares either, so I'll take it as a win.

The bar really is on the floor.

I'm just about to take the attention off me and ask Sloane to introduce herself when Veronica says, "Cool. I'm not autistic, so I know it's not the same, but if you ever want to rant about how confusing people are, just let me know. My sister is autistic so the two of us do it all the time, and I have a *lot* to say about that subject." She looks me right in the eye then, her gaze still sharp but somehow not as intimidating as before.

And I guess this is it, the moment I've been waiting for. Here, in this room, there's finally a person inviting me to talk about this part of myself. In an instant, there's so much I want to discuss with her, from my fear of not being likable enough because I don't understand social cues like other people do, to all the other messy feelings I've locked up inside my chest for so long.

Instead, the words that come out of my mouth are "I've heard there's a trauma dump scheduled in week two, though, so maybe we can unpack some things later. We have to save the big stuff for then, you know."

I don't even fully intend to say it, but those are the words that fill up the room anyway.

Veronica snorts. "Fair enough," she says, and normally I'd feel proud of myself for making somebody laugh, but right now, all I can think is that I've just ruined the perfect chance to really form a deeper connection with someone. All because I'm still depending on my reflex of steering the conversation in a less vulnerable direction.

*Is unlearning that reflex even possible at this point?*

The question floats through my head all night. It's there while Sloane introduces herself, telling us she's seventeen, used to play indoor volleyball, and lives in Belford—a town I know isn't that far from Willowmoor. It doesn't go away even as we divide the beds among the four of us and I end up in one of the top bunks. It stays with me as we turn off the lights and say good night, and even after that, it's still there, lying awake next to me while I wait for sleep to find me.

I don't know how much time passes as I stare at the ceiling in the darkness, thinking over every single thing I did and didn't do today, but when I eventually roll onto my side, I swear Sierra is looking at me. She's in the other top bunk, on the same level as me, and though it's hard to make out anything beyond shapes with the lights off, I can't help but feel like her eyes are on me.

*How am I supposed to do this?* I want to ask her. *How do I stop caring about people's opinions of me?*

But all she does is turn the other way, leaving me to figure out the answer to that on my own.

# 5. You Don't Have to Do Everything on Your Own

To my surprise, I'm not the most awkward person at the breakfast table the next morning. Sure, that might be because I've only added a grand total of ten words to the conversation, but at least I'm not doing . . . whatever Liam is doing.

Veronica, who is sitting to his left, turns to him. "Can I have the water pitcher?" she asks, her voice the most unsure I've ever heard it. Granted, I've known her for less than a day, but it seems out of character all the same.

Instead of passing it to her with a smile like I'm sure he would do for anyone else, Liam quickly grabs the water pitcher and pushes it into her hands, spilling a few drops on the table in the process. They don't murmur a quick "There you go" or even look at her.

Veronica frowns. "Thanks . . . I guess," she still says, but Liam has already moved on to ask Sloane how her summer has been so far. Sloane's eyes slide between Liam and Veronica in confusion before she answers the question, but Liam acts like everything about this is completely normal.

This tension has been hanging over our table ever since Veronica decided to sit down next to Liam half an hour ago. I don't think she recognizes him from school, but her presence alone has sent Liam into panic mode. He refuses to acknowledge her existence in any way, no matter what she does or says, and she's clearly picked up on that.

I wonder how long Liam thinks they can continue doing this. I hope not too long, since this morning already has me nearly overdosing on secondhand embarrassment.

Unfortunately, once we're done with breakfast and it's time to walk to the beach, it becomes hard for me not to focus on my own awkwardness. While the group has been jumping from one topic to another effortlessly, I've been quietly lingering beside them, listening to them crack jokes and say whatever comes to their minds. Some of it doesn't make any sense, like when Maya confidently says they'd be pistachio if they were an ice cream flavor, yet I'm still overthinking anything I want to add to the conversation in case it makes things weird. At this point, I'm even second-guessing what to do with my pinkie fingers, which is how I know I've really hit rock bottom.

It is interesting to observe the group, however. I notice that Noah is much louder and dorkier, perhaps, than he is at home. *Does he hide parts of himself, too?* I wonder, but I can't imagine it being true. Why would someone as amazing and likable as Noah feel the pressure to put on a mask?

Surely I'm just making things up.

I also notice that where Yasmeen is as calm and steady as the ebb and flow of the sea, Maya is an unpredictable storm, chaotic and unable to sit still. I've never believed that opposites can find a balance together—after all, there's always one side that overshadows the other, right?—but somehow the two of them make it work.

After fifteen minutes of walking, we finally arrive at the beach, and I'm no longer able to keep up with their pace. My footsteps automatically slow down because of the sand that quickly finds its way between my toes, and, well, it turns out the feeling is just as unbearable on the second day.

I'm the last one to arrive at the beach volleyball courts. Twelve pairs of eyes watch me as I struggle toward them. Right before breakfast, Adrian divided all the campers into smaller groups and assigned each group a main camp counselor as well as a slightly different schedule from the rest of the groups. As he himself so lovingly said, "It's the only way to make sure we don't have eighty loud teenagers in the same place at once. At least not all the time."

I ended up in a group led by Gigi, together with Sierra, Noah, Liam, Maya, Yasmeen, Sloane, Veronica, and four others who already seem to have befriended one another—Renée, Lynn, Samuel, and Louis. Daniel is in some other group, which is going to make it a bit more challenging to spend time with him, but relief fills my chest when I realize I don't have to face him just yet. At least this way, I can perfect the new version of myself before showing him I've changed.

"All right!" Gigi exclaims, dropping a bag of beach volleyballs in the sand. Her grin grows wider and wider with each passing second spent looking at us, almost as if we're magic in the making.

Then she says, "It's time to run some laps around the court."

I scan the reactions of the people standing around me. None of them groan in protest. Not Noah, not Maya, and certainly not Sierra. Yasmeen, however, looks just as thrilled as I feel—which is to say regret is written all over her face.

*Same, girl,* I want to tell her. *Same.*

Gigi claps her hands twice. "Come on! Let's do this!"

I put down the cold water bottle I was holding and pray there won't be too much sand sticking to it when I need it before following the rest of the group's lead.

It doesn't take long for Noah to slow down his pace a little to jog by my side. "Hey," he greets me. "How are you feeling?"

I keep my gaze on the uneven sand ahead of me, trying to make sure I don't lose my balance and fall face-first into it. "Right now? Feeling out of breath, mostly," I tell my brother. We haven't been able to talk a lot yet, but every small chance he sees to check in on me or make me feel included, he takes. It kind of makes me want to cry. Or rather, it makes me wish I *could* cry, just so I could show him how much it means to me, but in reality I haven't been able to shed a tear in years. Not since I got started with the rules.

"I just—*oh Jesus I can't breathe*—want to say I appreciate you looking out for me here," I say instead.

From the corner of my eye, I see Noah look over at me. "Of course," he breathes out softly, genuinely, but I have to stay focused, so I don't meet his gaze.

We jog around the court together one time, then another and another and another. At first, all I can think about is the goddamned sand beneath me, but as we go on and on, it gets hard to even feel it—or anything else, for that matter. All I know is that my heart is beating faster than ever and my lungs are aching, the pain getting even more intense each time I attempt to take a tug of air.

We keep going when my head starts spinning from running in circles, and we keep going even when I'm convinced I can't take another second of this. We keep going after that, too, all the way up until Gigi puts an end to my misery, announcing that we'll stop after one more lap.

"Nice," she tells us when we're done. "Take a quick sip of water, and then we'll start doing the real work! Woo!"

I almost huff at Gigi's words. *Surely whatever comes after this water break can't be worse than running that many laps,* I think. But a few minutes later, I find myself wishing we could go back to the good old times of running in circles.

Because "the real work" means playing beach volleyball, of course. During the warm-up, I might've been out of breath, but at least I knew how to not completely mess up. The same can't be said about this. I knew I wasn't going to be good, but I didn't expect it to be *this* hard to have some control over a ball.

Sierra passes me the ball, her movements so effortless and smooth that it looks like she was born to play this sport. Like she's been doing this since the moment she took her very first breath. I, however, try to push the ball back in her direction so she can smash it and end up almost breaking my fingers instead.

It feels that way at least.

Sierra still throws herself into the sand in hopes of saving the ball, but she's too late. It hits the ground right in front of her.

"Let's try that again!" Gigi encourages us, and so we do. Sierra serves the ball to Veronica and Sloane, who are on the opposite side of the net. The two of them run across the court and succeed at bringing the ball back to us.

No matter how short she is and how innocent she seems, Sloane sure does know how to smash. The ball spins into my half of the court, and I run after it, having to dive into the sand to get there in time. Somehow I manage to steer the ball in the right direction, toward Sierra.

*A win!* I think, too proud of this achievement to realize I have to get up fast, as Sierra is about to set up the ball so I can hit it back over the net. When I eventually remember what I have to do, it's too late. Sierra passes the ball perfectly, making it go higher than usual to give me time to get up, but still, I'm not on my feet in time.

The ball hits the ground. Again.

*Shit.*

I wait for Sierra to glare at me, for her neutrality to turn into frustration because I'm ruining this thing she loves, but she doesn't. All throughout practice, even when I make the same simple mistakes over and over again and can't help but curse myself, she stays focused on the ball instead of me.

That doesn't stop me from feeling guilty, though.

*Why did they ever think pairing the two of us up was a good idea?*

I'm tempted to ask Gigi on multiple occasions, but since she's busy giving me advice on how to get better at beach volleyball, I doubt she has time to deal with my insecurities, too. She takes me aside to teach me some of the basic techniques, like how to have the most control over the ball when passing overhead or underhand. Or how, when waiting for the ball to get to my side of the court, my feet should be shoulder width apart, and I need to bend my knees a bit, too, leaning forward so I'm ready to run after the ball if necessary. Gigi even teaches me that what I've been referring to as *smashes* are actually called *hits* or *spikes*.

Honestly, the terminology there is a bit disappointing to me. Especially given how this summer camp's name is literally SMASH! Who approved that?

By the end of practice, a blush colors my cheeks, both because of the workout and from how embarrassed I am to know so little about this sport. At least I'm a little less horrible at this whole thing now, but let's just say that doesn't mean a whole lot.

"Great work, everyone!" Gigi says, after which I internally grumble that she's a liar. I ignore my thoughts and focus on what she says after that. "We'll have lunch in thirty minutes, which means you get a little break!"

We walk back to the cabins, and I can already imagine what it would feel like to throw myself onto my mattress. It would sink a little, almost like a hug for my tired body. A hug that I really, really need right now.

*Luckily there are only a few more steps separating me from my bed,* I think.

But then Gigi walks up to me. "Hey, can we talk for a minute?"

I knew I wasn't going to be good at this whole beach volleyball thing, but I didn't think I'd be bad enough to need an intervention on the first day. I didn't even know it was possible to *be* that bad at a summer camp, but I must've broken some kind of record for sucking at volleyball.

I'll see it as an achievement, I guess.

"You can sit down if you want to," Gigi tells me, shutting the door behind her. The inside of her cabin is pretty much the same as the one I share with Sierra, Sloane, and Veronica, except for the fact that Gigi has this room all to herself.

Still, I take it in. She has certainly made herself at home here. The little shelf above the desk is filled with books, all their spines in different bright colors, and there are some pictures scattered through the room, too. One of them catches my eye, showing a younger Gigi pressing a kiss to a freckled, redheaded girl's cheek. Behind them is a sign that reads, in huge block letters, WELCOME TO SUMMER CAMP 2019!

I tear my gaze away, feeling like I'm intruding.

"So," Gigi starts once we're both seated, either not noticing or not caring what I was looking at. She leans toward me a little bit. "You go by Ellie, right?"

I try to ignore the way my heart hammers in my throat. *Can she send someone home?* "Yes, I do."

She nods to herself. "Okay." Then a smile. "How are you doing, Ellie?"

I can't even hide my confusion. I blink, then blink again, and again, and again. I expected a lot of questions, but that was *not* one of them.

Before I get to think of a response, Gigi blinks back at me. "Wait," she says, "you thought something bad was going on, didn't you? I really tried my best to not give off that vibe, but I'm *so* sorry if I scared you anyway!"

A little weight falls off my shoulders . . . until I realize I don't have a clue what else I could be here for. If there was bad news from back home, Gigi would've asked Noah to come with me, too, right?

I swallow. "It's totally okay, but, um . . . why am I here, then?" I ask.

Gigi smiles at me. "To answer my question, of course," she tells me, as if that clears anything up. Luckily, after a beat, she adds, "I know we don't know each other yet, so this might be considered weird, but I just wanted to check up on you. You're autistic, right? I was an autistic sixteen-year-old at summer camp once, too, so I get how overwhelming and lonely things can feel here, especially at the start."

My first thought is a panicked *What gave away that I'm autistic? Does she think I'm weird?* But then I realize it must be mentioned in my file or something.

I study Gigi for a second. I don't mean this in the "she doesn't look autistic" way, but I never would've guessed she is. She appears so genuinely happy and confident. Ever since I got diagnosed a year ago, I've been associating autism with having to be quiet and careful. To me, autism is something that means I have to constantly walk on eggshells to still be considered worthy.

But Gigi looks like she's just living her life, and she's still autistic. I like her vibe, and so do other campers, it seems. So why do I keep letting being autistic hold me back when I can own it instead? Like her?

I shift in the chair I'm sitting on, straightening my back and trying the words out loud, this time with intent. "Um, yes, I'm autistic. It's really nice of you to check in with me. I've . . . been better, to be completely honest."

I haven't stopped to think about how I've been handling things since the party, since the night everything blew up. I let myself be upset and scared for a few seconds, and then as soon as I came up with my plan, I focused on that instead. But now, I can feel it again. All those messy emotions. The fear that Daniel was right. The anger directed at him for barely even apologizing to me. The pain from holding the sharp shards of my heart together when all I want is to let myself fall apart just this once.

Instead of ranting about my life back home, the thing I tell Gigi is "I'm kind of scared I'm holding Sierra back. She's really good at this whole thing, and I'm, well, *not*."

Gigi nods to herself, considering what I'm saying. "I get why you feel that way—especially since Sierra has a lot more experience with this—but I think it will turn out just fine." She grins. "After all, you were paired together for a reason."

"Wait." I lean a little closer to her, curiosity getting the best of me. "What's the reason?"

"We think you'll work well together."

"Can you be a little less vague in your answer?"

Gigi's smile grows again. "No, I cannot. But I'm sure you'll see why we think you two will make such a good team soon enough." She leans back in her chair, studying me. "If there's something else you want to talk about, though, do let me know. Like I said, SMASH! can feel lonely and overwhelming, but I promise you'll find your place here soon. So? Anything you still want to discuss?"

I shake my head, and she nods.

"I'll see you at lunch, then?"

"Okay, see you in a bit," I say, getting up from the chair, then turning my back to her. My hand is on the doorknob when I realize something.

"Actually, there might be one thing I want to ask you," I tell Gigi, spinning around to look at her. She nods again, so I go on. "You seem to be so confident in who you are. How do I do that?" I break our eye contact. "I just mean . . . I'm having a hard time not caring about what other people think of me. You know, with all my autistic traits. How do you stop caring so much that you start to suffocate yourself?"

I kind of expect her to look at me like I asked her what the square root of 729 is, but Gigi doesn't even have to think over her answer.

"It's really hard sometimes, but I guess that, for me, it started with letting in one person who didn't judge me. They saw so many parts of me I was ashamed of, and then they showed me that . . . that maybe, it doesn't really matter if some people think of me as wrong, undeserving, or broken. Because I also have people who see me for who I really am—people including myself. That's what's most important to me now." She purses her lips for a second, thinking it over. "Does that answer your question?"

I nod slowly, still processing her words. "It does. Thanks."

Her smile returns again, and I decide right then and there that if there were ever a movie in which the sun is played by a human, my dream casting would be Gigi. Lighting up a room sounded unrealistic until right now.

"Good," she says. "Now get out of here! Go enjoy the rest of this break!"

"Will do," I tell her right before I throw open the door to her cabin . . . and collide with a whole human being in the process. I only just manage to keep my balance by grabbing the person's shoulder.

"I'm *so* sorry, I wasn't—" I start to say, but then I realize it's Sierra Levine steadying me and my apology becomes the last thing on my mind.

I let go of her, tensing. "Did you hear any of that?"

To my relief, she immediately shakes her head, frowning. "No, I wasn't eavesdropping or anything. I was just waiting for you to come out."

"Oh." I clear my throat. "Well. Here I am." I let out a nervous laugh, then follow Sierra as she starts walking. I rub some of the remaining sand off my arms, shivering at the sensation like I always do.

Sierra looks over at me. "You're really not a fan of sand, are you?"

"Is *anyone*?" I ask with another laugh, thinking that I've asked a rhetorical question. But Sierra tilts her head slightly, studying me with suspicion.

"We're at a beach volleyball camp," she points out.

I press my lips together. "Right."

For a moment, a silence stretches out between us. Then: "So . . . why are you here?"

I stop walking and turn to her, my mouth opening, but no sound comes out for a few seconds. "What? Sierra, you were *literally* waiting for me outside . . ." I manage to say eventually.

"No, I meant what are you doing here. At camp," she explains calmly. Patiently. No judgment for me misunderstanding her words. "Most of the time, people are either here to play beach volleyball or to have a fun summer camp experience with friends. I assumed you'd be here for the friendship part, but you're kind of . . . hard to read. Anyway, if you're actually here to play beach volleyball, I can help you practice," she offers.

As helpful as extra practices would probably be, I don't have time for them. I have to focus on my plan, after all.

"Thanks," I tell Sierra, "but as you said, I kind of dislike sand. So yes, definitely here for the friends part."

She takes me in then, considering. "Oh, okay. I just thought, since you've been pretty quiet . . ."

She trails off, and I stare at her, my lips parted a little as I'm at a loss for words. *Did she . . . did she study me?*

Upon seeing my expression, Sierra closes her eyes a second too long for me to consider it blinking. "Damn, I worded that awfully, sorry."

I shrug. It might've been a very direct statement, but that doesn't mean I see it as rude, especially not since she made a point with her observations, which I admit to her: "I guess I'm just not good at making friends."

For a second, I think she's going to sigh and say she knows what that feels like. *Maybe Liam and Maya were wrong about her,* I think. *Maybe she really does want to make friends here, but she's just scared or insecure or simply doesn't know where to start.*

For a second, I really do think Sierra is going to turn out to be just like me, but then she says, "Fair, I guess. I'm sure it'll turn out fine. Anyway, I stayed back to ask if you're open to doing those extra beach volleyball practices with me."

I don't even have to think about my answer to that. "Why would I willingly do that? Again, I don't even like sand. Let alone rolling around in it in hopes of not allowing some silly ball to drop."

"First of all, that's *not* what beach volleyball is about."

The corners of my mouth tug upward slightly. "Except it kind of is," I tease her, which she decides to ignore.

"We'd be practicing extra so we can win the competition at the end of camp, which, no offense, wouldn't be possible with your current . . . skills."

"No offense taken," I say, because it's not mean, just true. *But why do we want to win so bad?* I almost ask her, but then I realize that maybe it's a given for Sierra. She loves beach volleyball and wants to win this, so she's going to find a way to make that happen. End of story.

"Okay. Sure. I'll do it," I let her know, and even though she doesn't smile, her face lights up just a little bit. Like one cloud disappearing only to reveal it's still too misty for the sun to shine through.

"*But*," I add, "I would need you to do something for me, too."

She shrugs. "Sure, I guess that's fair. What do you want?"

I take a deep breath, thinking about what Gigi told me. All I need is to find one person who definitely won't judge me until I'm brave enough to open up to others, too. One person who I know I can't mess up around because there's no actual friendship at stake—because we're nothing more than two people helping each other out.

I meet Sierra Levine's eyes. "I need you to teach me how to be myself again," I say.

She looks at me like I've just demanded she kiss me on the mouth. "I barely know you, Eleanore."

"I know, that's why this is so perfect!" I exclaim, which only makes Sierra's frown deepen. I clear my throat, toning my enthusiasm down a bit. "All you need to do is talk to me until I learn to stop caring about what others say or think of me. I have a step-by-step list of things I need to learn this summer," I tell her.

"Oh. Um, yeah, I can definitely do that," she assures me. "So . . . we have a deal then?" she asks, arms crossed over her chest.

Immediately I offer her my hand, and after looking at it for a few seconds, Sierra shakes it. Her hand is warm, softer than I expected. Excitement fills me as we stand there, our hands meeting in the middle—because now my plan could finally start working.

I smile without even thinking about it. "Deal."

# 6. Remember to Not Think

"Eleanore? Do you understand?" Sierra asks for what could very well be the thirteenth time in the past ten minutes. She's been trying to further explain some of the basics of beach volleyball to me, and though she's certainly a good teacher, showing me exactly what I need to do with my hands to gain control over the ball, I still have no idea what I'm doing whenever she lets go of me.

Sierra sighs at the sight of my blank face.

"Right. Okay," she says. "Maybe we should just play and go from there." She throws the beach volleyball she was holding at me, and I manage to catch it before it can hit me in the face.

*Nice reflexes,* the voice in my head compliments me, but a second later Sierra murmurs something to herself and tells me, "You're not supposed to *catch* the ball. Just . . . pass it back to me, and we'll try to keep it up in the air for as long as possible."

I do as she says, throwing the ball upward, then quickly making a cup out of my hands and holding them above my head.

My fingers aren't too relaxed but aren't too tense, either. It's all about finding the perfect balance between those two, apparently. When the ball nears my face, I push it toward Sierra, and unlike yesterday, I don't feel like I've broken multiple bones in the process, which is progress, I guess.

It doesn't take long for the ball to hit the sand, though. But we try again. Again, again, again.

"Keep going," Sierra says after a while. By this point I've definitely broken my personal record. I'm a little out of breath already, my forehead covered in sweat even though I haven't been running around nearly as much as my partner. Sierra, however, doesn't seem tired yet, because right when I start to feel like I could become good at this, she announces, "Let's make this a little harder."

Just like that, she puts some more distance between us, taking quite a few big steps away from me before finally coming to a stop. For the first time in the history of ever, dropping headfirst into the sand is really tempting.

But the ball goes back up in the air, and somehow I find motivation to keep going. I stretch my arms out, bringing them together and angling them until they form a flat-enough surface to be able to guide the ball back to Sierra. It makes its way over to her in a close-to-perfect arc, giving her all the time in the world to pass it back to me in an easy way.

Instead, she spikes the ball, and I have to throw myself into the sand to save it from facing the same horrible fate.

Right as the ball hits me, I realize my arms are going to be unbelievably red by the end of this. Not from sunburn—

I applied lots of sunscreen, thank you very much—but from this girl's ability to smack a ball like it personally attacked her innocent grandma.

We go on like that for a long time, just passing the ball to each other over and over again, until Sierra dives into the sand in hopes of getting to my exceptionally badly played ball in time. Somehow, against all odds, she manages to keep it up in the air, but she does inhale a whole lot of sand in the process.

I rush to her side, leaving the ball to its own fate.

"Okay, okay," Sierra says through her coughs. I try patting her on the back, but she immediately waves me away. "We should probably take a little break."

"Or," I propose as we sit down on a bench, "we could just, you know, stop for today."

Sierra takes a long, *long* sip of water, and I almost dare to get hopeful. Almost. But of course, all she says to that is "Good joke."

"Anyway," she continues, looking right at me yet still ignoring my over-the-top pleading expression, "I was thinking that, to save time and all, we could use these breaks to work on that first goal of yours? So, for the next"—she glances at the time on her phone—"fifteen minutes, we can play a game that'll make you overthink less and say what's on your mind more. Sound good?"

Once I've nodded in defeat, she quickly explains the rules to me. "It basically goes like this: I ask a question, we discuss our answers, then it's your turn to ask something, and so on. Got it?"

"Loud and clear, boss," I tell her, "but isn't this game of yours just . . . having a two-sided conversation?"

"Last time I checked, *I'm* the teacher here," she reminds me. She takes another sip of water, this time a quick one, before she starts. "First question: Who is your favorite person in the world?"

I don't have to think about this too much. Even after everything—the distance and the hurtful comments—it will always be Noah. "Definitely my brother," I tell Sierra.

She waits for a second, and another, and another. For a moment, I wonder if, to an only child, it's weird to be close to your siblings, but then she finally asks, "That's it? That's all you have to say?"

I avoid her brown eyes as she arches an eyebrow at me. "You promised not to judge me, Sierra," I say.

"I'm not judging," she tells me, holding her hands up in the air as if claiming her innocence. She's quiet. Then she sighs. "Okay, I see. Now, why don't you ask a question next?"

I press my lips together for a second. "Okay. Um," I say as I'm thinking of what to ask. Eventually, I offer, "What's your favorite color?"

Immediately, Sierra raises an eyebrow at me. *Again.* "What is this? Get to Know Each Other: Kindergarten Edition?"

"Hey! Stop judging! Simple questions can lead to meaningful conversations, too," I argue. "Maybe there's a really sentimental reason why you like a color, or maybe it just really matches your vibe. Who knows if you don't ask?"

"*Sure*," she says, stretching out the sound in a way that lets me know she absolutely does not agree with me. "I just like green because I like green, though. Nothing more to it than that."

I smile at her, knowing exactly how to corner her here. "Which tells me you're a very no-nonsense type of person."

She rolls her eyes at me but decides not to discuss this further—I assume because deep down she *knows* she's lost. I'm a second away from flashing her a victorious smile when Sierra sighs and says, "Just tell me the oh-so-deep meaning behind your love for your favorite color."

She looks at me as I let a silence fill the air between us for one, two, three seconds. Then longer and longer and longer until, after a while, she breaks it to say, "You can't seriously be overthinking what your favorite color is . . ."

"I'm not!" I assure her, an unnecessary blush warming my cheeks. "I'm overthinking what to say *about* my favorite color. Which is red, by the way."

"I know. You make that abundantly clear with your outfits," she says dryly, even though I miraculously haven't worn anything red at camp yet. *Huh.*

She takes me in for a moment, her eyes scanning me from my face to my shoulders to my hands, which I'm nervously playing with. She's concentrating so hard that I can't help but wonder what Sierra sees when she looks at me.

Am I that girl from back home, the one she remembers passing in the hallways at school? Am I a person she'll get to know better now, someone who could eventually become a friend, even though she's not looking for one? Or am I just a burden to her, too? The girl who's making her summer at beach volleyball camp harder than it should be?

I look at her, trying to read what's on her mind. But I don't even know what *I* see when I look at Sierra, let alone what she thinks when she sees me.

Suddenly she gets up, and I tear my gaze away from her, scared I've made her uncomfortable with my accidental staring. "Break is over," she lets me know.

I stay put, my eyes widening. "Um, I was promised fifteen whole minutes—not seconds."

For the first time, I see something close to a smile on Sierra's face. Not necessarily because of her lips but because of the spark in her eyes. *Glad to see my misery is so amusing,* I almost tell her, but before I can open my mouth, she shakes her head.

"Just get up, Eleanore."

And even though every single muscle in my body protests, I do.

She passes the ball to me, and our game picks up right where we left it. Only this time, Sierra doesn't stay silent as we play. "So," she starts, "it's my turn to ask a question now. Tell me: What's something that makes you feel totally at ease?"

I stay quiet, partly because I'm confused about what exactly it is that she's doing and partly because I'm busy chasing a ball. She'll have to wait for my answer until I have more room to breathe, I decide, but then Sierra yells, "You have three seconds to speak, or I'll spike without even a hint of mercy!"

She starts counting down, and I can't believe I'm saying this, but hearing Sierra Levine scream the word *spike* at me is the most terrifying thing I've ever experienced. Normally when looking death in the eye, I freeze, but right now?

I pass the ball back to her again and quickly say, without

thinking it over properly, "I GUESS I FEEL MOST AT EASE WHEN WRITING IN MY NOTEBOOK."

The ball returns to me in a nice arc. I let out the breath I was completely aware I was holding, thinking for one peaceful moment that the coast is clear, but then Sierra demands, "Tell me more. What do you write?"

I'm just about to quickly shout the first answer that comes to mind again when she adds, "And *please* don't scream this time. I can still feel your last words echoing in my ears."

"Okay," I say, trying to stay focused on the ball while also talking in a calm and collected manner. "Well, I like planning. And making lists. And—I don't know—even just writing myself vague notes I won't know the meaning of two days later. It might be weird"—I hit the ball—"but looking at my own life on paper makes me feel like I'm in control of it. Even when I'm not."

From the corner of my eye, I see Sierra nod. "Things are always less complicated in theory."

"*Yes*," I say, breathing the word out in relief that she understands. "Well, most things, at least. Not chemistry."

Even though I don't have time to look at her, I like to imagine Sierra has traces of a grin on her face then. "Definitely not chemistry," she agrees. "Okay, next question—"

"No," I interrupt immediately, surprising both of us.

"What do you mean, '*no*'?" Sierra asks, letting the ball that's coming her way drop in the sand. "Eleanore, I know you don't exactly like playing volleyball, but this is actually working. You're finally starting to get out of your own head."

And she's right. By trying to keep the ball up in the air and talk at the same time, I can't focus as much on saying the right thing. There's just no room for that in my head anymore. But still I repeat, "No. It's not time for the next question." I meet her gaze. "You have to answer your own question first."

She rolls her eyes at that. "This is an exercise to help *you*, not me, but sure." She sighs. "I feel at ease when I'm playing volleyball. Beach or indoor—it doesn't really matter. Although I do personally prefer the rules of indoor volleyball, but whatever," she says, and even though she tries to brush over that quickly, my eyes are widening already.

"There are different rules?" I interrupt.

She raises an eyebrow at me. "You really don't know much for someone whose brother plays, but yes, there are a few rules that differ. That's something to go over when you are more familiar with beach volleyball, though. We don't need you to confuse the rules right now."

I nod. "Fair point," I say, even though I wish I could get her to elaborate. For some reason, I want to know what exactly she prefers about the indoor volleyball rules—not so I can see which I would prefer but simply for the sake of knowing something real about her, however small it might be.

"Anyway." Sierra pulls me out of my thoughts. "I know most people don't understand why it's so relaxing to me since volleyball can get quite exhausting and intense, like any other sport, but . . . I don't know. I quit playing indoor volleyball a few months ago, and before beach volleyball season began, I was the most restless I've ever been." She pauses to think. Then: "Even though playing means I constantly have to be moving and thinking about my next moves before even doing my first, it's relaxing to me. When I'm on a volleyball court, the rest of the world disappears. It's just me and my team."

I nod, considering her words. "It does sound kind of nice, you know, when you put it like that. It almost makes me want to play." I give her a grin before fully processing what she said. "But why did you quit?" I ask carefully.

She shrugs as if it's nothing important. "Let's just say that Willowmoor's team is a little too homophobic for my liking, and I have yet to convince my dad it's worth it to play in another town." Before I get to ask anything else or even say I'm sorry people are so awful, she picks up the ball again, holding it under her arm.

"You're actually pretty good at this. You've got more instincts for playing volleyball than you think," she tells me.

I straighten my back automatically, the corners of my mouth lifting into a proud smile.

"*But*," Sierra continues, "there's still a lot of work to be done. Come on."

She throws the ball back in the air, and so the game continues.

The next evening, after a long and hot day at the beach practicing with Sierra, I try to make some progress in the book I'm reading. I'm not exactly succeeding at it, given the fact that I've been staring at the same page for five minutes now.

The author is describing the butterflies the main character feels when she thinks about the love of her life. It's poetic and probably at least a little bit exaggerated, but as I close my eyes and picture Daniel's face, I don't feel even a fraction of what is being described.

Again and again, I imagine kissing him or holding his hand or, I don't know, falling asleep while I'm comfortably wrapped up in his arms. But when I inhale sharply, it isn't because the thought of him is taking away my ability to breathe. I'm just frustrated by the lack of progress I've made so far, by the numbness in my chest that's too similar to how I felt whenever I kissed Daniel in the past. There was never anything poetic about it—no fireworks exploding in the sky when our lips met, no warmth spreading through my body, no feeling of coming home. Just two lips meeting until it was done, as if we were checking the same item off a to-do list over and over again. Three seconds of happiness because you finished the task, always followed by the return of that numbness.

*There has to be more to it than that, right?*

A loud and unexpected knock on the door of cabin 4 brings me back to my current reality.

I exchange some looks with my cabinmates, but they seem just as clueless as I am. It's Sierra who eventually moves to find out, while Sloane, Veronica, and I steal unsubtle glances at the door. I really don't know who I expected to appear, but it certainly wasn't my ex-boyfriend.

Daniel stands in the opening of our cabin, brown hair still

wet and a little wild from a shower. I've been thinking he might spend this whole summer pretending we don't know each other, but now, when his blue eyes find mine, he doesn't look away.

"Hey," he says, putting his hands in the pockets of his black sweatpants—the only thing he's wearing right now.

"Please put a shirt on," Sierra orders by way of greeting. "And then go back to your own room. All right, good talk, bye!" She immediately goes to close the door again, but despite being caught off guard by her boldness, his eyes widening, Daniel still manages to stop the door with his foot.

"Stay out of it, Levine. I'm here to talk to Ellie," he tells her, words sharp as a knife. Then he looks back at me, softening. "Do you want to come take a quick walk with me?" he asks gently.

I put down the book I'm holding, carefully sliding a bookmark between the pages to win myself some time for thinking of what my answer should be. This is exactly what I wanted, right? Daniel is *finally* showing some interest in me again.

So why do I wish Sierra would just slam the door in his face?

I push that thought away. It's probably just my hatred for confrontation. "Alright," I agree, "but you better make it quick, because the chapter I'm reading is *really* good."

He smiles, watching as I climb out of the bunk bed.

"I'll be right back," I whisper to Sierra, who looks like she's still considering shutting the door in Daniel's face.

She doesn't, so I step out into the evening air and shut the door behind Daniel and me instead.

It's a hot summer night, the sky above us a warm shade of

orange as the sun goes down, but there's a cold breeze that makes me wrap my arms around my body.

"So . . . how've you been?" Daniel asks as soon as we've started walking.

I turn my head so I can look at him, my eyes sliding from his dark hair to his perfect jawline and back up to those blue eyes that always have a mischievous spark in them. It makes him look alive, like he's constantly up to something.

As I take in my ex-boyfriend, I can't help thinking that he's handsome . . . but that's just the problem, isn't it? I know he's attractive, and yet for some inexplicable reason, I can't *feel* it. Not in my heart, not in my belly, not anywhere. Except for in my head.

*Give it a chance,* I urge myself. *You're trying to change. Maybe he will, too, and everything will make sense this time.*

"I've been having an incredible time here. Like, the people are really nice, and I can't believe I'm actually saying this, but . . . I'm starting to not hate playing beach volleyball. I think . . ." I start, then I trail off before continuing with "I think I might even miss all this when we have to leave. Although I do think some rest would be nice." I laugh.

Instead of replying to any of what I just told him, Daniel nods slowly. Then, after a quick pause, he stops walking and turns his body toward me. "Listen," he says, "I am so incredibly sorry for what happened at the party." He takes a deep breath, his Adam's apple bobbing as he swallows. I force myself to look him in the eyes, waiting to see if I can find sincerity in them.

But I've never been good at reading people.

"I know there's no excuse for my behavior from that night," he continues, "but I need you to know I would do anything to go back in time and not say what I said. It's just that . . . drunk me was upset and confused about why you were so chill about me breaking up with you. I thought it meant you never liked me at all."

I tense at those words, immediately wanting to deny what he's saying—so quickly it almost seems like a reflex. But before I get to make out a single word, Daniel continues talking like this is some kind of monologue instead of a two-sided conversation.

"I now know how stupid that was, so, what I wanted to say is: I know I messed up. I was drunk, and I said some horrible shit, but I'm sorry for that. Every single word."

A silence hangs between us as we walk side by side and I think it over.

Eventually, because I don't know what else there is to say, I simply admit, "Okay. I appreciate you . . . saying this." No matter how bitter the taste in my mouth still is when I think about what he said, for my plan to work, I need to forgive Daniel.

Even if the guy really doesn't know how to apologize properly.

"Yeah? Awesome," Daniel says, clearly hearing only what he wants to hear. "I guess I'll just walk you back to your cabin, then?"

"Um, sure."

It takes us only a minute or so to arrive back at cabin 4. A minute I spend entirely focused on the presence of Daniel walking next to me. A minute I spend willing butterflies to flutter around in my chest at his proximity.

It doesn't work, but maybe I'm thinking it through too much.

*Yeah. That must be it.*

I'm about to tell Daniel good night when he grabs my wrist and says, voice low, "There's one more thing I need to discuss with you, actually. I saw you at the beach today and . . . Don't get me wrong, it was nice to see you happy, but are you, like, *actually* friends with Levine?"

I frown. "Yes, I am," I lie. "Is that a problem?"

Daniel finally loosens his grip on my wrist. "Just . . . be careful around her, okay? I know how important your reputation is to you, and hanging out with Sierra is not going to help with that."

I tense at his words. There's a truth in what he's saying, for sure, but all I can focus on right now is the sudden anger in my body. I want to snap, want to tell him, *Oh, but you saying I'm boring in front of everyone was* so *good for my reputation, right?* I almost open my mouth before my eyes meet his, and then I can't help but chicken out. His eyes are so familiar, such a big part of the old Ellie's life that I can feel myself turning into her again. The girl who wouldn't dare to speak up.

I look away, telling Daniel, "I'm always careful."

He nods to the door of cabin 4, apparently satisfied with my answer. "I'll let you get back to your night, then. And to your book. I'll see you around, though?" he asks.

I almost nod, almost let him turn away, before I realize I have not once asked him a real question in this whole conversation. How is he supposed to see that I've changed if I revert to who I always was around him?

I quickly think back to what Sierra taught me and blurt out, "Actually, I need to know something, too."

Daniel looks at me, his interest regained. He loves the chase most of all—a challenge, a mystery to figure out—so I decide to give him something to think about.

Before the moment passes and Daniel gets bored, I ask, "Do you have a favorite color?"

For a moment, he just blinks at me. Again, again, again, like he's so caught off guard by my question that he's forgotten how to frown.

I tilt my head at him, signaling that I'm waiting, which makes him snap out of it. "It's blue," he says. "Why do you need to know that?"

I think it over for a second, trying to find meaning behind his answer like I did with Sierra's yesterday, and even though I can't come up with anything, I smile like he's just given me the most interesting piece of information ever.

"Okay. In that case, I'll see you around," I tell him right before I disappear into my cabin, leaving him outside with just enough questions for me to stay on his mind for the rest of the night.

# 7. Never Wake a Girl Up at an Ungodly Hour

Now that I've been doing extra practices with Sierra for a few days, I have four pages in my notebook filled entirely with things I've found out about her.

For starters, she's incredibly patient, but that's mostly because she's stubborn as hell. Once she's set her mind to something, she will do absolutely everything within her power to make it happen. Whether that means winning the end-of-camp beach volleyball competition or helping me be true to myself or even just keeping that stupid ball up in the air—it doesn't matter. Sierra Levine never does things halfway. When she wants something, she's always going to give her all.

Secondly, I've noticed that she does, in fact, smile. She just tries to hide it for some reason. But even if she doesn't let her lips curl up entirely into a wide grin, there's this spark in her brown eyes whenever she's amused. The same spark that was there the six times she did accidentally let a laugh slip.

Not that I've been keeping count or anything.

There's also the fact that she always makes sure she has her hair up in a ponytail. I'm literally sharing a cabin with her, but I still haven't managed to catch her with her hair down. She's always dressed before the rest of us wake in the morning, and at the end of every day, she lets her hair loose only once the lights are out. At least, I hope she does. Sleeping with a ponytail in doesn't exactly seem comfortable or healthy to me.

My list goes on and on, and I guess that, after what she did an hour ago, I have another item I can add to it: Sierra Levine is absolutely ruthless.

"So . . . what is your dream job?" she asks as she casually passes the volleyball back to me. Like she doesn't understand that I'm going through literal hell right now.

"You woke me up at six a.m.," I remind her. Then I spike. As hard as I can.

Sierra catches the ball even though we both know she could've easily played it back to me. "First of all, nice work," she compliments me. "That was a good one. But, second of all, you really can't keep using that as an answer to every single question I ask you. You know that, right?"

My lifeless eyes meet hers. "You. Woke me up. At *six a.m.*"

Sierra forces the corners of her mouth not to lift, but I notice that she wants to laugh either way. It's in the way the corner of her mouth twitches, which is such a small thing, barely noticeable, and yet . . .

Even with all my current moodiness, there's something satisfying about being the reason she almost smiles. Like finally checking off the hardest item on my weekly to-do list.

I'm distantly aware of the fact that I'm now full-on staring at her, but I couldn't bring myself to look away even if I wanted to. The sight of her in the golden morning sun is something straight out of a painting. I'm no artist, but even I feel the urge to capture this moment, if only to bottle up the calming warmth that fills my belly.

But then Sierra frowns and the strange feeling fades away, leaving me with nothing but an embarrassed blush coloring my cheeks.

"You okay?" Sierra asks.

Finally I find the strength to look away. "Um, yeah," I say. "Just feeling a bit funny, I guess."

Sierra nods, and this time, she's the one studying me. Her expression doesn't give away what's on her mind, but as her brown eyes take me in, I feel as though she's lighting a fire within me.

I can't decide if I like that or not.

"Maybe we should stop for now," she says eventually, crouching down and passing me my water bottle. "And please make sure you stay hydrated. I've barely seen you drink anything yet this morning."

"Will do, boss," I assure her, trying to shake the feeling of her eyes on me as I drink. I've just swallowed the water down when my throat instantly grows dry again.

While I take another sip, Sierra packs up our stuff, after which we start our short walk back to SMASH! I thought campers weren't allowed to be left unsupervised, but for some reason Sierra's dad didn't seem to mind much.

I don't know what to think of that yet, but I guess it's convenient for these extra practices.

When we get back to SMASH! we find a bunch of people already waiting for breakfast to start. My friends spot the two of us and immediately wave us over, even though they're sitting at our usual table and I would've found them regardless. Before I can make my way over to them, though, Sierra pauses in front of the glass door separating us from the rest of the group.

Her brown eyes meet mine so intensely, I have to look away. "Are you sure you're feeling okay?" she asks quietly, as if this is something that should stay between us and us alone.

I'm about to nod and tell her not to worry when my gaze accidentally lands on Daniel. I think back to our walk yesterday, of how much work I still have to do to fix this whole mess, and suddenly I don't feel so okay anymore. I swallow at the reminder of everything that's at stake.

"I will be," I quickly assure Sierra. "Just have to eat something first, I guess," I lie, and then I open the glass door and walk up to my friends, Sierra trailing closely behind me. For a moment, I really do believe she's going to take the chair next to me—the one that's always left empty. But then she walks right past it, wordlessly deciding to sit down at a small empty table in the corner instead.

*Right.*

I have no reason to be disappointed by this. I knew going into this that Sierra would never consider the two of us friends, even if she became the person I'm most myself around, and I was fine with that. I *am*. But I can't help that my heart—that treacherous little thing in my chest—sinks a bit as I see her walk away from me.

It's not that I'm hoping we'll hang out with each other a lot after this summer. I'm not letting myself be *that* naive. Still, that doesn't mean I haven't been enjoying her company or hoping she would stay in mine for now, as long as we're here. Because even if what happens at camp stays at camp, I thought we could at least enjoy the little time we have here together.

But I guess that, even at camp, we're nothing more than two strangers helping each other out, counting down the days until we can go back to living our lives without each other.

The next day, my whole body is sore and I have a Headache that's worthy of that capital *H*, but that's not going to stop me from staring at my phone while lying in bed. Pictures of my classmates flash before my eyes, all of them showing off their bright smiles and cool adventures and amazing friends. I quickly scroll past most of them, but when I see that Nina has posted some truly stunning pictures of herself posing in Willowmoor's local flower garden, I make sure to give it a heart.

Barely ten seconds later, a string of notifications pops up on my phone.

NINA ❤:

THANK GOD

you're finally online!!

i've been bored out of my mind

YOU:

surely it's not that bad?

NINA ❤:

girl . . .

it definitely is that bad

She's quiet for a moment, then suddenly she's typing again and the following messages pop up:

i can't believe you actually abandoned me

to play volleyball no less

ugh

My thumbs move on their own, typing an apology to Nina almost as a reflex. Probably because it *is* a reflex, but at the last minute, I manage to hold myself back. I pause for a second before I hit the delete button repeatedly, only stopping once the message box is completely blank. Then I start writing something entirely new. Something the Ellie of a few weeks ago wouldn't have dared even *thinking* of sending to someone.

It's strange, typing out a message in which I talk about no

one but myself. But it's time for me to start actually using the things Sierra has taught me beyond the bubble that is summer camp, so, without too much overthinking, I hit send.

i didn't expect this either but it's actually been really fun so far haha!!

the people here are so nice :)

and in my defense we do a lot outside of playing beach volleyball too

this evening we had a quiz night for example

I'm still typing out a follow-up message to tell her I almost ended up in last place when Nina's reply comes in.

**NINA ❤:**

wow

sounds like you're having a good time

meanwhile i am over here DYING from boredom because you left . . .

Maybe she doesn't mean it in a hurtful way, but after reading her words, my shoulders slump instantly and I stop typing—stop moving, even. As if I truly believe that if I make myself smaller, if I don't take up too much space, Nina won't be annoyed with me anymore.

That is, if she's truly annoyed in the first place. I'm probably just reading too much into her message. After all, that's what I always do: I overthink stuff and try to find meaning where there isn't necessarily any, but . . . I don't know. Whether intentional or not, it stings, especially coming from the person I call my best friend, the one who is supposed to make me feel like I'm the best version of myself. But instead her words are a reminder of why I started following my seven rules in the first place. A reminder of the consequences attached to forgetting them.

I swallow, deleting the half-finished sentence I wanted to send before replacing those words with what I know Nina expects me to say.

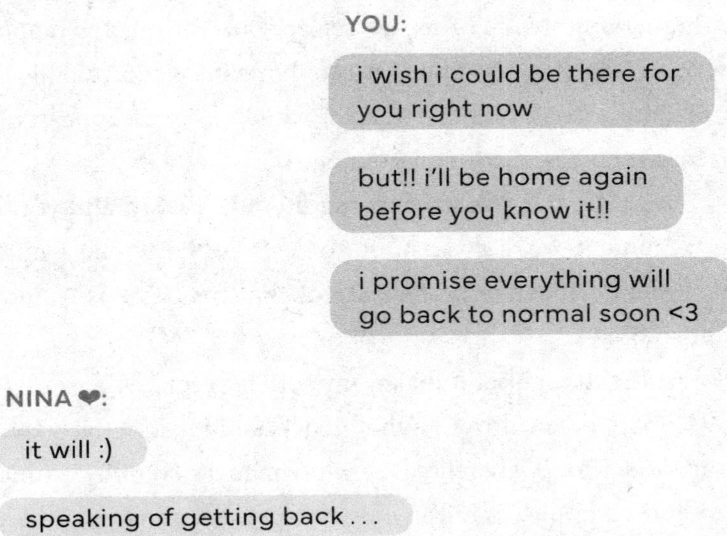

how are things with you and Daniel?

Before coming to summer camp, I told Nina I was hoping to win Daniel back. She was delighted to hear it, seemingly unbothered by Daniel's earlier behavior. It stung for a short moment that she wasn't angry about it anymore, but her approval made me feel a little bit better about my plan. Now, though, I wish I'd never told her about it. Lately we haven't had a single conversation that didn't end with her bringing him up. The subject has exhausted me to the point where all I tell her now is that we went on a walk, just the two of us, a few days ago. She sends a few exclamation marks in response, and then I tell her I have to go help my cabinmate with something. Before she can reply, I make my phone's screen go dark, returning to the here and now of a quiet cabin 4, where no one actually needs my help with anything. None of us are asleep, but Veronica is tapping away on her phone just like I was only seconds ago, and Sloane is reading a book on her e-reader, while Sierra disappeared to go for a "short run" over an hour ago.

I don't get her. We are moving literally all day, and yet the very moment we're given time to rest—at 9:00 p.m., I might add—she decides the perfect use of that free time is to move some more.

Just the thought of it makes my sore legs ache.

A groan breaks through the silence, and I instinctively think to apologize for it when I realize who made the sound: Veronica.

"Someone please tell my sister to stop watching so many

romance movies. They're *definitely* rotting her brain," she says, putting her phone away as well. "Like, she just sent me pictures of herself sobbing over *10 Things I Hate About You.* Not only is it a typical romantic *comedy*, but it's one she's seen a thousand times by now." Veronica stares into the distance, her face drawn in a frown that means she's either disgusted, confused, or perhaps both at once.

Sloane puts down her e-reader for a moment, asking what I'm wondering as well. "Why does that upset you?"

"Are you kidding me?" Veronica instantly replies, her green eyes wide, as if she can't believe we even have to ask. "Movies like that seriously lack depth and originality. It's always the same: A girl meets some guy, they fall in love, they mess up, and oh! Wait! They make up with some spectacular grand gesture, and everything is absolutely perfect forever and always!" She rolls her eyes. "Spoiler alert: That's not how real life works."

I shift on my bunk bed carefully, but the wood beneath me still creaks a little. As if my accidentally making a sound means I have something to say, Veronica and Sloane both look up at me expectantly. "No," I agree softly, "of course that's not how real life works. I don't think anybody is claiming it does. It's just a common misconception that—"

The cabin door opens, causing my voice to falter.

"Hi," Sierra says upon seeing we're all looking at her. She's a bit out of breath. She takes off her headphones and shoes and, without another word, climbs onto her own bunk bed. There, she lays herself down on her back, breathing in and out, in and out.

I'm still focusing on the rhythm of her breathing when Sloane breaks through the silence. "What were you going to say, Ellie?" she asks me gently.

"Oh." I clear my throat. "It really wasn't important. Don't worry about it."

Veronica frowns. "Bullshit," she says. "I want to hear what exactly this misconception is, so bring it on."

She keeps looking at me, urging me to finish what I was saying, and so does Sloane. I bring my gaze to my hands and allow myself to ramble.

"I just meant to say that the end of a movie isn't the end of the characters' lives per se, you know? Whether you give a movie a happy ending or a sad one or something in between, realistically there's always going to be ups and downs after it. And as for rom-coms being cliché and lacking depth . . . I feel like people just want an excuse to look down on the genre. Sure, rom-coms *can* be cliché, and sometimes some more depth really wouldn't hurt, but that's an issue with the writing of that movie—not with the genre as a whole. If someone personally doesn't like rom-coms or, I don't know, *fun*, maybe they should just say that instead." I shrug. "That's all."

It's silent in the room for a bit after that, but not in my head. I start internally cursing myself. Truly, *why* did I have to say all that? Nobody actually cares about my opinion, and now the people I'm supposed to befriend think I'm weird and talk too much and will regret ever asking me to speak up and—

"I hadn't thought about it like that." Veronica nods slowly, considering my words. "Yeah, you definitely have a point there. From now on, I'll just have to tell people I hate fun."

She says it with a completely straight face, but her words make Sloane burst into laughter. "I'm sorry!" Sloane wheezes, tears quickly starting to gather in the corners of her eyes as she keeps laughing and laughing and laughing. "It's just that—" she tries, then stops to laugh some more. "We've only known each other for a few days," she eventually says, "but that's the most *Veronica* thing anyone's ever said."

By the time she gets the words out, I've stopped holding in my chuckles, mostly because Sloane's laughter is so contagious. Veronica just looks between the two of us. "I feel like I'm being laughed at right now," she says, but a small smile is tugging at the corners of her mouth, too.

I shake my head. "No, no, don't worry," I reassure her, trying to calm myself down. "Anyway, I assume I don't have to ask *you* this, Veronica"—another laugh escapes me—"but, um, Sloane, do you like rom-coms?"

A part of me expects her to give me a short answer and then end the conversation, but instead she says, "Duh!" and picks up her e-reader again with a smile. "I am literally in the middle of reading one right now, and there's dozens more on this thing." She taps the screen of the e-reader and shows us the books in her expansive library. Most are indeed romance novels if I'm correctly judging them by their cute covers—something I most definitely do.

"Oh, this one's my favorite, though," Sloane lets us know.

Then she starts explaining what it's about with so much passion that I have to hold myself back from grabbing the e-reader out of her hands and reading the book myself.

"You guys *have* to read it," she finishes, at which I promise I will and Veronica says, "I think it's best for both of us if I don't, actually."

Sloane studies her, then shrugs. "Okay, fair enough. What's your favorite book, then? Some dark, depressive tragedy, I assume?" she says, wiggling her eyebrows with a smile.

"Eh, I'm more of a nonfiction type of reader, actually. So unless you think life is a dark, depressive tragedy, then no."

"Okay, that's really cool, though. I've barely read any nonfiction," Sloane replies before looking back up at me. "What about you, Ellie?"

"Oh, I read a lot of romance as well, but I'm too indecisive to have one absolute favorite," I say, almost waving it away. But there's something in the way Sloane is looking at me, with her open and kind face, that gives me the courage to elaborate. "Every time I finish a book I love, it's my favorite for a while, until I read another one, and so on."

I show them my recent reads, after which we go through our reading histories together, comparing what we've read and going on about books we hate, love, or still want to read. Sometimes we all agree with one another, but more often we don't, which makes it all the more fun. I even end up climbing out of my bunk bed to join Veronica and Sloane on the floor so that talking to each other is a bit easier. And also so I can be in the front row to watch how Veronica's face scrunches in playful discomfort as Sloane narrates a kissing scene from her current read.

Sierra is quiet the entire time, but even so, I catch her constantly looking over at us from the safety of her bed, her face unreadable—as always. Maybe she's judging us in the hopes that we stop talking, or maybe she's trying to think of a way to join in on our fun. I'm not quite sure, but I think of asking her if she has a love for books or movies or anything, just to make sure she doesn't feel left out. But when she catches me looking back at her, she quickly moves her gaze elsewhere, so I leave her alone. I make myself focus on Sloane and Veronica and our rambles instead of the mystery that is the way Sierra Levine feels about, well, anything.

The three of us stay up far too late, the exhaustion I was feeling earlier nowhere to be found as the conversation flows and flows and flows.

For once, I let it.

# 8. Don't Underestimate the Power of Faking Confidence

Gigi asked us to do one simple thing: Pick a team name for the game of capture the flag we're going to play tonight. There's so little at stake here, and yet we've been brainstorming a name for five minutes now—without any success.

"Oh!" Sloane gasps, looking at our team, which consists of the same twelve people we have practice with every day. "What about Let's Hit It? Or Here to Serve? Get it? Because we play volleyball?"

Maya thinks it over for a few seconds, pressing their lips together before shaking their head. "Hmm . . . no. That's not quite the right vibe. It's already much closer than We Ball, though," they add, turning to look at Liam with their eyebrows raised.

Immediately he holds up his hands to defend himself. "Listen, it was a joke, okay? By now you should know not to take me too seriously." Their mouth twitches as they attempt to hold back their smile, but some laughs still escape.

Maya tries to swat him, but he sees it coming and dodges. "You're such a menace." Maya sighs.

"And you love me."

"I'm having a hard time remembering why, but I do, yes," Maya shoots back, not letting a single beat pass.

Liam's lips part again, and I honestly think that if we'd let them, he and Maya could banter like this forever. Luckily, Samuel, a person in our group I don't interact with as much, puts an end to it by clearing his throat.

"Can't we just pick something like that as our team name? The Menaces?" He shrugs as everyone looks at him. "I don't know, it seems kind of fitting."

One of his close friends, Renée, snorts at that, but Maya clearly doesn't take it as an insult. "It's perfect," they breathe out in wonder.

"Finally," Gigi exclaims as we confirm our group will be called the Menaces for tonight. "This was starting to get painful to watch. But now that that's settled," she quickly adds, "it's time for you to make another decision. God help me."

There's a collective groan, which makes Gigi shake her head fondly. "This one is actually necessary for playing capture the flag, though. I want you to hide this"—she takes a small green flag out of her pocket and waves it at us—"somewhere. It can't be inside any of the cabins, and it should be on your half of the playing field, but other than that, you have free rein. Just try to make sure your opponents won't find it.

"The other team has a blue flag they'll be hiding, too, and to win this game, you'll have to find theirs before they find yours," she further explains. "When you're on their side of the playing field, the opponents can tag you, which means you have to freeze wherever you're standing. You can be freed only if someone from your own team tags you again. The same goes for when they're in your playing field, of course, so you'll have to both defend and attack. I recommend dividing your team into those who will try to find the other flag and those who will protect your own flag." Gigi takes a deep breath. "Are those rules clear?" she asks, and once we've all nodded, she exhales again. "Great! Then you can go hide your flag now. The game will start in ten minutes."

Gigi hands the green flag to Noah, who is standing closest to her. She smiles as she tells us, "Good luck."

And so we begin walking around, trying out several hiding spots. We put the flag down behind some of the many trees surrounding our cabins and even try to shove it underneath one of the small white cottages, but the spots all seem too obvious.

"I have an idea," Samuel says, reaching out his hand to Noah. My brother puts the flag into his open palm, and without further explanation, Samuel starts to climb the tree we're standing next to.

His second foot has only just left the ground when Liam breaks through the silence, yelling, "UM? THIS DOESN'T SEEM VERY SAFE?"

Veronica's hands fly to her ears at the sharp sound, and she glares at Liam. "Your screaming isn't exactly helping when it comes to his safety. Plus he seems to know what he's doing," she says, but of course Liam ignores her, just like Samuel ignores his comments.

"YOU COULD GET HURT!" Liam tries again.

"Veronica's right. He clearly knows what he's doing. As long as he doesn't go too high, it should be fine," Noah tells them.

This time, by some miracle, Liam actually lets it go, sighing. "Fine." Still, they watch Samuel with anxious, wide eyes, swallowing hard.

"Sure. Why don't you just ignore me. *Again*," Veronica mumbles next to me, quiet enough so that I know Liam won't have heard her.

My first instinct is to comfort her. To wrap my arm around her shoulders and say I'm sure it's not personal, but the truth is that I still don't know exactly what Liam's deal with her is. I've only heard Liam's perspective—how Veronica goes to his school and doesn't have the best reputation there—but other than that, I really don't know anything. Especially anything that could help her feel less shitty.

Besides, hugging Veronica seems even more risky than usual right now. Her jaw is set, and there might as well be flames in her green eyes. It's as if she could snap at any moment.

Meanwhile, Samuel keeps climbing until he's several feet above us, totally unbothered by all the chattering below him. When he stops, it's so he can tie our green flag tightly around one of the tree's branches. "There we go," he says, and then he climbs down before jumping out of the tree and joining us on the ground again. He looks up at his work with a smile.

It would be hard to notice the flag if I didn't know it was there, especially since the color is so close to the shade of the leaves that surround it. "This is genius," Maya exclaims, something I can only agree with. "Like, *damn*, Samuel, you're on fire today."

He smiles at them. "Thanks."

About five minutes later, when we're back in the middle of the playing field with Gigi, our opponents arrive. They've called themselves the Red Flags, even though their flag is blue, and they consist of twelve fit white guys around our age. And, of course, standing in the middle is Daniel Solomon, wearing the biggest grin of them all.

One look at him and I can hear his voice in my head saying, *She's just another cute but boring girl* over and over and over again until it gets hard for me to swallow. Until it feels like something is pushing me into the ground and all the warmth in my body has left me. It's probably taken the color in my face away with it, too, because Sloane asks quietly, "Hey, are you feeling okay?"

I turn to her, blinking until she's in focus. "Yeah, it's fine," I tell her, waving it away as if I don't feel my stomach turning anxiously.

"Alright," Gigi says after asking both teams if we're ready. "That means the duel between the Red Flags and the Menaces starts in three . . . two . . . one . . . GO!"

She claps her hands as hard as she can, and immediately chaos ensues. People begin to run around, some already chasing each other in hopes of making them freeze, while I sprint to the opponents' side of the field. There, I decide to hide behind a bush until things calm down a bit. Noah follows right behind me.

The two of us sit there in silence, not wanting to make a sound and risk revealing our location to the Red Flags. Eventually, though, we seem to be the only ones still close to the border, so we dare to walk around, trying to figure out where Daniel and his teammates hid the blue flag.

"You've been spending a lot of time with Sierra," Noah observes out of nowhere.

"Oh. Yeah." I swallow. "It's actually been really nice," I tell him simply, because I can't reveal the actual reason for my hangouts with Sierra. Knowing him and his protectiveness over me, he'd immediately try to talk me out of wanting to get back together with Daniel.

Luckily, Noah nods, not questioning a single thing. Instead he shoots me a small smile. "Good. You deserve nice, accepting, decent people in your life. Ones who live nearby. And who don't constantly make you feel bad about yourself or—"

I give him a look, making him stop. "She really isn't that bad," I say.

"Yet you know exactly who I'm talking about," he counters.

I shake my head at that, trying to ignore the thousands of buried thoughts about Nina I've collected over the years. Thoughts about how she speaks like she doesn't realize people around her have feelings, too. Thoughts about how she's only actually nice to me when I fit into her expectations of me and how, once I don't, she makes me feel small. Like she did when I was texting her a few days ago about how I'm having fun at SMASH!

In moments like that, she makes me feel like I'm nothing but a burden to her. Sometimes I even find myself wondering if she likes me at all or if she's still just trying to get Noah to notice her through my friendship.

But even with those flaws, Nina is still a good friend, right?

She might not be perfect, but in the end, she'll always have my back. I need to be more grateful for that.

"How are things between you and Sloane?" I ask, keeping my voice low so she doesn't overhear.

Noah immediately drops the previous subject. "Why? Has she said anything about me?"

I stop searching for the flag to give Noah another look. "As far as I know, you two are the neurotypicals here, so I think it's best if you just communicate with each other and *not* through the autistic girl."

Noah blushes, turning back to me with a smile. "I guess you're right."

Our conversation is cut short when we hear voices in the near distance. I hide behind another bush, and, again, Noah follows, crouching right next to me.

"Are you sure it's a good idea for us to stay this close together?" I whisper.

Noah raises an eyebrow at me. "Ellie, come on. I've played this game every single summer for years now. Trust me, I'm an expert."

He's barely able to finish that sentence when Daniel and some other guy suddenly appear and run toward us. At first I'm not sure they've seen us, but then they get close enough for me to make out Daniel's grin.

*Shit.*

I get up and start running as fast as my legs allow, while Noah does the same—luckily in a different direction this time. As expected, the nameless dude chases Noah, which means . . .

I look over my shoulder, and of course, there Daniel is, bounding after me as I run without a clear idea of where I'm going.

"Ellie!" he yells when I focus on the path in front of me again. I don't look back anymore, scared he's gaining on me with every second that passes. It sounds like he is. "You don't actually think you can outrun me, do you?"

And the thing is, I don't. There's not a single doubt in my mind that Daniel will be able to tag me in less than a minute, especially with the way my lungs are burning and my heart is hammering in my chest. I really, really don't stand a chance against Daniel.

I have to try, though. If only to surprise him so he sees I'm not as boring as before.

"Watch me," I tell him as I start running a little faster, praying to anyone who will listen that I can keep up this pace.

Even as my breathing gets quick and short, I don't stop. I don't stop when I spot Sierra at some point, and I certainly don't stop when Daniel keeps talking to me, trying to trick me into giving up. I don't stop until I feel a tap on my shoulder, and even then, I stop only because I don't have a choice.

As I slow down and freeze, Daniel stays with me. It feels like it's been ages since I've been able to study him up close. He's wearing that grin again, showing his straight white teeth as he ruffles his fingers through his brown hair. He takes a step closer to me, blue eyes staring into mine. I force myself to return his gaze, waiting for warmth or a spark or anything, really, to find its way into my belly like it would if I were watching this scene in a movie. He looks at me, I look at him, and we're the only ones who matter in this moment. But that thought is more terrifying than it is exciting.

*Soon,* I promise myself. *Soon you'll be able to fall for him.*

"Come on, Ellie," Daniel says. "I know you hate games like this. Just tell me where you guys hid that flag and I'll put a quick end to this so you can go back to your night."

Still holding his gaze, I lift the corner of my mouth just a little, making his eyes drop to my mouth briefly. Then I shake my head.

"In your dreams."

He sighs. "Fine. Have it your way. But we both know it only takes one look at your team and one look at mine to know who's going to win this. It's as predictable as it gets."

With those words, he runs back to where we came from, leaving me to stand here on my own. At least, for about ten seconds I think I'm alone, and then I hear someone make a gagging sound behind me. A short tap on my shoulder follows, freeing me.

I turn around to see Sierra standing there, her face drawn together in genuine disgust as her eyes point in the direction where Daniel disappeared.

"What an asshole," she mumbles. "Why would you ever date him? You're—"

I avoid looking into Sierra's brown eyes, scared of what she thinks of me. Instead I study everything around me as if this is the most interesting forest I've ever seen. I look at the clouds in the sky and the trees surrounding us and even the grass beneath my feet . . . until my gaze falls on a dark blue something. I can't help but interrupt Sierra by gasping. "Oh my god."

I quickly run toward the blue flag that's been tied around the base of a lamppost, pulling at the fabric until it's free, after which I yell, "FOUND IT!" as loud as I can.

Everything but the blue flag in my hand disappears for a second. I don't think about how much work I have yet to do this summer, or about what will happen once I return home, or even about what Sierra was going to tell me only seconds ago. The only thing on my mind is the fact that we won this game. I beat Daniel.

It's such a small, silly thing, but for one simple moment, it means the world to me, filling my lungs with a hope that I breathe in and out.

Noah finds us first, cheering as he sees my big smile. He's followed by Gigi, who officially confirms we've won. More people make their way over to us, some of them on my team, others on the opposite side, and eventually Daniel returns, too.

I can't help but smile at him, still holding the flag. "Guess we're not so predictable after all, huh?"

We spend that evening commemorating our victory with a walk on the beach. Although it definitely doesn't come close to my idea of a celebration, I let my gaze travel across our current view, actually . . . enjoying it. Sure, I still don't get why people like strolling their feet through sand so much, but I must admit there really is something about taking a walk on the coast when it's dark outside. During the day, there's loads of people who laugh and chat while screeching seagulls fly overhead. Right now, at night, though, there's nothing but the sound of rippling water filling my ears and the sight of the softly lit-up moon hanging in the sky.

It's the kind of view that makes my heartbeat slow down. The kind of place I can picture people visiting so they can whisper secrets into the night.

That's not exactly what we're doing right now, though.

"Elle Woods is a lesbian, and I am ready to die on that hill," I hear Maya tell Liam after he briefly brought up *Legally Blonde*. "Damn, I hope someone at college allows me to write an essay about that," they say, more to themself than to anyone else. "I would absolutely nail that."

Even in the darkness, I can see Yasmeen smile. "I honestly have zero doubts about that. You're very persuasive, you know. The only question is . . . will you be the Vivian to my Elle?"

Maya gasps dramatically, turning to their girlfriend with a matching grin. "Babe, of course I want to quietly yearn for you until it kills me. I thought you'd never ask!"

"Get a room, you two," Liam jokes as he looks over his shoulder. "I feel for Renée and Lynn, to be honest. They must be third- and fourth-wheeling in your cabin so bad."

At that, Veronica decides to join in on the conversation, too. "You do realize that metaphor does not make sense in that situation, right? A lot of vehicles actually *need* four wheels."

There's no real bite or judgment to what she's saying, only teasing, but Liam doesn't look her way at all. They simply act like they didn't hear a thing. As usual. "Oh well," they try, scrambling for something new to say.

I'm wondering how much longer it'll take for Veronica to snap when she cuts Liam off.

"No. Don't *oh well* me again. God, I'm so sick of pretending not to notice this!" she exclaims with a frustrated groan. Her previously teasing tone is sharp as she looks right at Liam and asks, "Tell me, where does this deep hatred you have for me come from? Because as far as I'm aware, we didn't know each other before this summer, yet you've been ignoring me since the start of it."

All of us are quiet then as Liam tenses at her words, not daring to look at her as he continues walking. The rest of us don't try to pick up the conversation we were having. It's as if each one of us freezes at the confrontation, even though we should probably just let Liam and Veronica figure it out together—without us awkwardly lingering beside them.

"Wait," Liam says slowly, holding eye contact with her for only a millisecond before he lets his gaze travel elsewhere again. "You . . . don't . . . know me?"

Veronica frowns. "Of course I don't. Just like you don't know anything about me, either."

"Oh." He clears his throat. "Well. We, um—we go to the same school, actually."

*And there it finally is.*

Veronica's mouth opens in either surprise or understanding or a mix of the two, but she quickly recovers, going back to looking like she doesn't care about a single thing in the world. One of her eyebrows shoots upward. "So? My previous point still stands. We don't know each other, so whatever you've heard about me being some kind of massive bitch might not be true at all."

Liam swallows. "Your friend group literally outed someone last year, though," he says. "And even within that friend group, you're not exactly known as a sweet angel, which, well . . ." He trails off.

I try to keep my face blank, but it's hard not to curiously glance at Veronica's face. I might not know her well yet, but I just can't picture Veronica doing something so messed up.

"I had nothing to do with that!" Veronica exclaims in her own defense, her voice loud enough to make me flinch. "The moment they told me what they did, I told them off. That's why those girls hate me now," she explains. When Liam doesn't react to that, she raises her chin and takes a step closer to him, adding, "Listen, I know I'm not always the friendliest person. I'm direct and honest, and yeah, I might be considered rude sometimes. But trust me when I say there are far worse people in our town than the bitchy girl who calls people out on their bullshit."

Before I've really processed what just happened, she's storming off, leaving angry footsteps in the sand. All I know is that my heart is beating too fast, and the more I focus on its rapid speed, the faster it seems to become.

Maya is the first to break the stunned silence hanging over our group. "Well," they say, stretching out the sound, "I think we should all be bitchy girls who try to call people out on their bullshit." They pause, brow furrowing at their own joke. "Except for the girl part, that is."

Everyone ignores them for a moment, instead eyeing Liam, who looks an awful lot like a loading icon with his lips parted. Then he slowly shakes his head. “Oh god. I need to go after her, don’t I?” he asks.

Nobody gives him an answer, but he knows it all the same.

“Shit. I, of all people, should know not to listen to what everyone at that stupid school says without second-guessing them. Fuck.” Liam sighs. “I should at least hear her side of the story, right? I’ll be back in a few minutes . . . I hope,” he tells us. Without waiting for a reply, they jog after Veronica.

As I breathe in and out, in and out, I wait for Maya to crack a joke or say something completely random that will launch us into a whole new conversation again. They’re really good at that, I’ve noticed. Jumping from one topic to the other until you’ve lost track of what exactly they’re talking about.

But now Maya stays quiet. The only sound comes from the ebb and flow of the sea and from me swallowing hard, but neither sounds are loud enough to drive away my anxious thoughts.

Luckily, that’s when I realize that I’m able to break this silence, too.

“I wonder why people here are so different from those at school and back home.” I sigh, pushing my own thoughts away.

Everyone’s heads whip over to me, but it takes a little longer for someone to speak up. It’s Sloane who eventually answers: “Honestly? I was just wondering the same thing. Being here feels like I’ve, I don’t know, escaped to some kind of different world? One where I actually belong?”

It comes out like a question, like she's not quite sure she's making sense, but then Maya nods reassuringly. "Yeah, I get what you mean. I've rarely felt as safe as I feel when I'm here."

"You know," Noah begins, voice soft, "I used to think that way, too, but then I started to see the familiar faces here, and . . . I don't think I still believe it's the people who are different. They're almost exactly the same, except for the fact that the people who make high school so miserable *aren't* the leaders here. At this place, the people who normally hide in the shadows to protect themselves get to live a little without constantly being judged. Because there's no one to set rules and ruin the safe spaces here."

He looks at me for only a second, but I know he's not just saying this for Sloane. His words are directed at me, too.

"That's the smartest thing you've ever said," Maya tells him, and he shakes his head, throwing it back in a laugh.

"Thanks? I guess?"

Sloane stares at the sand below her feet as she thinks Noah's words over, then looks back up with a sad smile. "I guess you're right, indeed," she says, taking a deep breath. "Living in the shadows really can serve as a form of protection. I kind of miss being able to do that these days." She pauses, then explains, her voice shaking a little, "Ever since I . . . since . . . last summer, people just keep staring at me. They're always watching what I'm doing. I don't know if it's out of fear or pity or judgment, but I hate every second of it. I just want to go back to how things were before they found out."

When she pauses, my brother says, "Hey, you can tell us

anything, but if you don't want to or aren't ready yet, that's okay. There's no pressure at all." He puts his hand on Sloane's shoulder and squeezes it lightly, but she shakes her head.

"It's fine. I really want you to know. For someone to know and not judge." Noah rubs her back, giving her the strength to go on. "I was, um, hospitalized last summer. That's why I disappeared and had to cancel my plans to come to SMASH!" She clears her throat, trying to swallow down her emotions, but they come right back up, audible in every word she speaks. "I was diagnosed with bipolar disorder a long time ago and have been taking meds for it for a while, but yeah . . . Things got really bad last summer, so then people found out, and now I'm no longer just the quiet girl anymore; I'm the bipolar one. Which is fine and all, but . . . I just wish they'd accept me as I am instead of thinking of me as broken."

A single tear rolls down Sloane's cheek. She wipes it away immediately, but more keep falling now, especially when Noah pulls her into a hug and lets her head rest on his shoulder.

"Can we do anything for you, Sloane?" Maya asks. "Because if I have to burn down a city for you, just say the word and I will do it. Well, metaphorically at least." They smile. "*Or* I can just tell you how worthy and wonderful you are over and over again, of course."

A soft laugh escapes Sloane, but still she shakes her head. "I think . . . I think I'd like to not feel alone in this right now. In being judged about my identity."

Yasmeen is the first to speak up at that, telling us all about her experiences wearing a hijab in high school. From teachers demanding she take it off to students telling her it's so sad that she *has* to wear a hijab because of her, and she quotes, "misogynistic religion." It's as if they forgot that there's a possibility that it is, in fact, *her* choice to wear one. Because she wants to. Because it's important to her.

After that, Maya reflects on what it's like to be a nonbinary lesbian of color at high school. "It's like people think I'm too many things at once. Indian, nonbinary, *and* a raging lesbian? Impossible, right? They want me to pick just one struggle when life doesn't work that way at all." They sigh, shaking their head, then letting out a snort. "If only they knew I have ADHD, too. But yeah, I don't miss high school even one bit. I just hope college will be at least a little better."

Sloane has stopped crying. She's still leaning on Noah, seemingly exhausted, but I do think this really helped comfort her—even though hearing about how badly our friends have been treated is incredibly frustrating, too. It's just nice to know you're not the only one going through this. That the problem doesn't lie with you, because other wonderful people who deserve better go through it, too.

*You can share your story as well,* I remind myself. But even though I'm no longer that scared of opening my mouth thanks to Sierra, getting vulnerable still feels like something foreign. Like a language I haven't spoken in so long that I've slowly started to forget the words.

Luckily, I know just the way to fix that.

# 9. Play by the Rules . . . of the Game, I Mean

This idea definitely sounded a lot better in my head.

"So let me get this straight," Sierra says from the other side of the tiny room. She's sitting cross-legged on her bunk bed while I'm lying down in mine, eyes pointed at the ceiling. "You want us to fall in love? With each other? By answering thirty-six questions? No offense or anything, but there's *no way* I'm doing any of that."

Heat rises to my cheeks as it hits me just how awfully I phrased my plan. I prop myself up on one elbow. "That—that's not what I meant," I assure Sierra quickly, trying not to pay attention to the way my heart squeezes when she exhales in relief. I gulp. "These questions help some couples fall in love according to people on the internet, sure, but in our case, we can just use them to help me open up. It's a way for me to learn how to be vulnerable around people again."

*And being vulnerable will also allow me to fall in love with Daniel eventually,* I remind myself.

Sierra studies me for a second, dark eyes scanning my face skeptically as if she's looking for a reason not to do this. She reaches my lips and pauses for a fraction of a second before sliding her gaze up to my eyes, nodding. "All right, then. Let me see that list."

I turn on my phone, which still has the article listing all the questions open. When I hand it to her, dangling over the edge of my bed, Sierra's fingers briefly brush mine, and the touch sends a surge of energy through me. The kind that has me unable to sit still any longer. I need an outlet for the adrenaline rushing through my veins.

*I must be really nervous about this.*

Luckily, I'm wearing a ring I can stim with. I slide it off my finger, twist it around in my hand, and put it back on. As Sierra starts reading aloud, I keep this pattern going.

"First question: Given the choice of anyone in the world, who would you want as a dinner guest?" She stares at the screen, frowning. I see its reflection in her brown eyes. "I don't see how this could ever make people fall in love."

"It's a good thing we're not doing that then, right?" I joke. "Either way, if I could invite literally anyone, I think I'd go with Iris Blackwell. She's this YouTuber who makes short films, and she's a huge advocate for autism acceptance, so I think I could learn a lot from her," I explain.

Sierra straightens her back. "I watched one of her videos. I think it was called 'Party Tricks'? It was beautiful . . . and also queer, right?"

"Oh yeah, very queer," I agree with a soft laugh before every muscle in my body tenses. "Not that it was *too* queer or anything. I mean, there's no such thing as too queer! People who truly believe stuff like that should go outside for three minutes and take a look at how heteronormative everything around us is," I ramble, only pausing because Sierra is pressing her lips together tightly to hide her laugh.

"What?" I ask, the corners of my mouth lifting despite my confusion.

"Nothing." She shakes her head, still trying to hold in her chuckle even though she knows I've noticed. "It's just kind of, um . . . *endearing*, for lack of a better word, whenever you defend yourself like this. You always assume you messed things up even when I didn't interpret your words in a bad way. Really. I assure you, non-autistic people don't think things through nearly as much as you do." She sighs. "Sometimes I wonder if the world would be a better place if we did."

"Allistic," I tell her, at which she tilts her head in a question. "That's the word for people who aren't autistic," I clarify.

"Allistic," she repeats, nodding. "Noted." Then: "I'd probably want to have dinner with Nina."

She watches me closely as she says it, awaiting my reaction, which comes in the form of a confused frown. "Wait. Nina as in my Nina? Why?"

She rolls her eyes at me, but I know by now that it's playful. "Let's just say I have my reasons."

"And what might those reasons be?"

Sierra shakes her head at the sight of me and my big, curious smile, but the left corner of her lips is ticked up into a barely noticeable grin. "Probably not what you're thinking."

The smallest blush colors her cheeks, and all the thoughts in my head come together in one big *Oh*. Who would've thought Sierra Levine had a crush on Nina Davis? Not me, that's for sure.

I feel my cheeks get redder, too. "I can't promise you a dinner with her, but I could get her to talk to you when we're back home, you know. We could make it a part of our deal."

Sierra thinks that over for a second. "Um. Yeah. That'd be great, actually," she says, and before I get to add anything else: "Next question."

Sierra's tone is final, but even if it wasn't, I wouldn't need to be told twice to drop this subject. For some reason, thinking about Sierra and Nina together makes something in my stomach twist uncomfortably.

We answer the questions in chronological order, covering topics from how we both don't like being the center of attention to our idea of a perfect day—which we agree is about the feeling, not the exact things you do—to so many other things. We talk about dreams and memories, and somehow, as time passes, it feels like we're sitting closer to each other, even though we're both still on our own bunk beds . . . too far apart from each other, in my opinion.

"Take four minutes and tell your partner your life story in as much detail as possible," Sierra reads aloud. She immediately shoots me a look. "You're not actually going to time this, right?"

"Oh, you know I will." I grin, reaching my hand out for her phone since she's still holding mine to read the questions.

She makes a noise to protest, but after a second she gives up, tossing me her phone and telling me her passcode so I can unlock it. I don't mean to seem like I'm snooping through her phone. I really don't, but I can't help but notice some things, like her background, which is a simple picture of a beach volleyball in the sand. Or a widget on her screen that shows her habit tracker, which includes only volleyball-related things.

"I mean this in the least offensive way possible," I start, "but does your whole life consist of nothing but volleyball?"

Sierra swallows, completely silent for a moment. She stares straight at me and blinks—again, again, again—until I'm just about to apologize for being so invasive. That's when she sighs, hesitant. "Go ahead. Set up a timer, and I'll tell you a story."

She watches me press start, then takes a deep breath, and finally she looks away from my gaze. "Once upon a time, a volleyball player was born. Not a girl or a child, but a volleyball player from the moment she took her very first breath. Just like her father.

"Luckily, she grew up to genuinely love the sport with all her heart, and soon it became her passion because of that love, but also because she noticed the way her father didn't really pay attention to her until she was on the court with their family name on her back. So she started practicing more. Playing well felt like the only way she could get him to be proud of her. And what daughter doesn't want her father to be proud? Especially when said daughter's mother is suddenly . . . gone."

My heart stops at her words. Right. How could I forget? When Sierra lost her mother to cancer two or three years ago, everyone in town knew about it, including me, but somehow I never connected that Sierra to the one sitting in front of me now.

Before I find any comforting words to say, Sierra continues talking.

"Eventually, practicing became more important than the few friends she had at school, so she lost them. It didn't matter, though. She had her teammates, and that was all she needed. really. But then, *somehow*"—the word comes out so sharp, I hold my breath—"they found out she likes girls, which made them feel so uncomfortable that they pretty much forced her to quit the team. Just like that, she was alone. It was too late to make new friends by then since everyone had already formed their cliques. Even worse was that she lost the spark of pride her father used to have when he looked at her."

Sierra turns her gaze back to me, smiling sadly. "There you go. That's my story."

I blink and blink and blink, half expecting this version of Sierra to dissolve. But it doesn't. Because she's real.

I never expected her to be insecure about anything, especially not something like this: who she is. She always seems so unbothered by the opinions of others, so sure of herself and her worth, yet here she is, showing me a whole other side of her. A side I never thought I'd see.

There are so many parts of Sierra Levine I haven't seen yet—that I will probably never get to see—but here, in this room, I feel a strange urge to change that. I want to know her below the surface. I want to know her fears, her dreams, her passions, and I want to know what makes her break into a smile so I can make sure that happens over and over again. I want to know who hurt her, and I want to know how I can take some of that pain away—even if it's just temporary.

Right now, I want to hug her.

Without thinking twice, I get up, careful not to hit my head on the ceiling as I shuffle toward the edge of my bed, ready to climb into Sierra's. But then I look up and find her staring at me, completely frozen except for the fact that she's blinking in confusion. I pull back right as the timer goes off, startling the both of us. I almost manage to fall in between the tiny space between our bunk beds.

"What exactly were you doing?" Sierra asks me once I've regained my balance and turned the timer off.

I look away, embarrassed by the fact that I was convinced this was a good idea only five seconds ago. "Sorry, sometimes I forget people can't read my mind and don't have the context I do. I just—you look like you need a hug, but I totally get it if you mind—"

"I don't," she interrupts quickly. Then she relaxes. She gestures for me to join her on the bed, which I do, but not without a very necessary blush coloring my cheeks because of her eyes on me. She takes in each of my movements. I get closer until, finally, I have my arms around her.

It's weird but also nice. Something I'm not used to but would like to be. She rests her head on my shoulder and hugs me back, and even though there's still quite a bit of space between the two of us, I feel like this is the closest I've been to someone in ages.

"I'm forcing you to be my friend now, you know," I tell her, feeling her heartbeat against my chest.

To my own surprise, she doesn't protest. "Okay," she whispers as she lets me hug her. When we both let go, she avoids my gaze, simply saying, "Your turn."

I take a deep breath, resetting the timer before delving into the story of my own life.

"Once upon a time, there was a girl with too big of a heart," I tell Sierra, following the same format she did. Somehow, opening up about my life as if it's a story makes it easier. Less real. "It might seem like a gift, to be able to feel everything so deeply, but to her, it was a curse. Because while her brother, her other half, fit into the world effortlessly, every small thing was a big struggle for her, and though she would never be upset with him for that, she became mad at . . . herself. Why, if he could so easily make friends and have conversations and be *normal*, couldn't she?

"A few years passed in which the girl held her breath so the people around her couldn't see her heart beat. She didn't care that it meant suffocating herself. Or at least, that's what she told herself and her therapist. But the latter saw right through her and told her she's autistic and that she's far from alone in that.

"Those words didn't matter to the girl at first. They didn't solve her problem at all. But then she spent the summer in a new place and took a risk: She opened up her heart for the people there. Eventually they made her realize she had started her story all wrong. So . . . maybe I should rephrase it.

"Once upon a time, there was a girl with a big heart, and though the many judgmental people around her made it seem like a curse, it was a gift. Because, as she realized, it's what made her *her*." I smile a little. "Though I suppose that ending is still a work in progress."

Now that I'm done, I wait for Sierra to tell me it was weird or ridiculous or just plain crazy of me to hold in my breath for so long, but instead she says, "You'll get there." She inhales deeply. "I'm sorry people made you feel like you had to do all that, though. I know it's easier said than done, but you don't have to prove to them that you're worthy. You know that, right?"

I look away. "I do have to, though. If I want to get through my senior year without too much drama, I'm going to need to prove I'm not as boring as Daniel told everyone I am. So I need to win him back."

"Oh" is Sierra's initial reaction to that. She stares at me for a full ten seconds before mumbling, "God, what an asshole. I seriously don't know how you put up with him for, like, half a year. Or more importantly: *why*."

I almost tell her that I felt like dating Daniel was something I was supposed to do, something I was expected to do because a cute boy was showing interest in me. But I bite my tongue just before the words slip out. Saying that would make it sound like I don't actually want to be with Daniel, which is *not* the vibe I want to give her—or anyone, for that matter. In the end, I just shrug, hesitating before I say, "The two of us make sense together."

But even at that answer, Sierra shakes her head. "No, you really don't. I mean, a week ago I probably would've said you did. You're the popular girl and he's the popular guy and all, but . . . no. Just no."

My heartbeat picks up in my chest, as if it's trying to run away from someone—from something. I don't want to know what Sierra means by this, don't want to hear her say that she realized I'm not the perfectly nice girl she thought I was. I don't want her to tell me that I'm not worthy of a guy who's as well-liked as Daniel, and yet I find myself asking, "What changed between a week ago and today?"

Now it's Sierra's turn to shrug. "You're just not who I expected you to be. Unlike the crowd you hang out with, you actually give a shit about other people."

Sierra's lips part to tell me something else, but she's interrupted by loud laughter coming from outside, where people are enjoying today's break in the sun. It's weird. I almost forgot there was a world still spinning beyond this room. A world beyond Sierra and me.

When the giggles fade, all she says is "Next question, then? Tell your partner what you like about them. Be very honest this time, saying things you might not say to someone you've just met."

She puts the phone down, leaning back curiously as she waits for me to give her my opinion.

"Well," I say, trying my very best to hold her gaze, "I like your honesty. Whenever I talk to you, there's no nonsense or pretending. You just say what you mean, which is something I really, really admire."

Sierra nods. "Thank you. That's really nice of you to say."

"I'm not done yet, Sierra," I let her know. "In fact, that's only the beginning of what I admire about you. Like I said, you're honest, but you also know when to mind your own business and let people live their lives. You are thoughtful and accepting and funny, and there's something comforting about your presence that I can't really explain but appreciate *so much*. You just . . . calm me down, in a way." I look away from her intense brown eyes, focusing on my hands instead, which I'm intertwining nervously in my lap. "But most of all, I like that you're a wonderful person. Even with all your grumpiness and sarcasm and sharp edges, you are kind. Not deep down; I don't have to search for your kindness. It's just there because that's who you are."

I feel Sierra's eyes burning right through my skin, but for some reason I can't lift my head to meet her gaze again. After a bit of silence, she softly asks, "Are you done now?"

I nod, waiting for her to say my rambling was too much or that I got her all wrong, but the thing she tells me instead is "I like how much you care."

At that my head snaps back up, and I look her in the eyes. "What?"

"I said I like how much you care," she repeats, voice soft. Genuine. "About everything. You deeply care about your brother and your friends and all the other people around you, even if they don't deserve you sometimes. Most of the time, actually. You're funny and literally the best example of a good person I've ever met."

She opens her mouth, then closes it, only to part her lips again and say, "In all honesty, I'm not that good with words, but just know there's so much to like about you. The real you. I don't think you should hide that person at school anymore. You like my honesty, right?" Once I've nodded again, she takes a deep breath and continues, "Then I'll just say it: The people at school are always going to find a way to say shit about you. No matter how perfect you are, they will find something to complain about. Look at Daniel, for example." She huffs in frustration, mumbling something that sounds a lot like "*that asshole*" under her breath. "You were the ideal girlfriend every guy always says he wants. Practically a manic pixie dream girl. You didn't complain, didn't ask for a lot of attention, and, well, look at you," she says, looking anywhere but at me as we both blush. "You were everything guys like him ask for, yet he still dumped you and called you boring in front of half the school. Nothing you do will ever be good enough for people like that, but that doesn't mean that you aren't. You *are* good enough," she says, meeting my gaze again and leaning in to show me how sincere she is. "In fact, I think you're fucking fantastic."

I hear her words perfectly, but it takes a little longer for their meaning to hit me. "Oh." I breathe out then, feeling like she just found the key to my heart and handed it to me instead of taking advantage of it. If I still knew how to cry, I'd probably burst into tears right now, but that's something I haven't been able to do in three years. "How did you know exactly what I needed to hear?"

I don't expect her to actually answer that question, but she does, shrugging. "I didn't know. I just wanted to tell you the truth."

A few more questions on the list pass just like that, until we finally reach number thirty-six.

A silence fills the space between us now that the very last question has been answered, but for some reason, I'm not freaked out by it. I don't want to run from this because there's an understanding in the air between us. Like she knows me and I know her and there's nothing we need to do except just *be* in each other's presence.

It's comfortable. New. Exciting, in a way. And I think that maybe . . . maybe it wasn't so ridiculous of SMASH! to team the two of us up after all.

Half an hour later, Sierra and I are lying on her bunk bed, which I'm starting to realize was most definitely not made to fit two people. We're not touching, but her hips are only one simple movement away from mine, and I'm increasingly aware that if I were to take my eyes off the ceiling and turn my head just an inch, the two of us would be nose to nose. We're already in each other's personal space, but I should probably get up before I accidentally do touch her and things between us turn uncomfortable. Still, I don't move. I'm not ready to leave this moment. Something about being so physically close to her feels . . . vulnerable, almost. Like we're sharing the same little bubble.

I can't bring myself to pop it just yet.

We've been quiet for some time now, but then Sierra's voice breaks through the silence. "How did you get into Iris Blackwell's videos?" she asks softly. The question is so sudden, I can't help but wonder what she's been thinking about to lead her to this. "I mean, she's known within queer circles, of course, but I never hear other people talk about her," Sierra adds.

If I could, I'd shrug, but I don't want to risk crossing the thin, invisible line between us. "I don't know. The algorithm just . . . brought her to me one day, and I happened to click on the video," I say truthfully. "Looking back, it's as if YouTube knew I was autistic and decided I needed to be educated on it before I even got diagnosed." I laugh, the sound merging with that of the door to cabin 4 suddenly swinging open.

Immediately I straighten my back, putting space between us with such speed that Sloane and Veronica might think Sierra's touch has burned me. I don't even know why I do it. It's not as if being in Sierra's bed is some sin they've caught me in, yet heat still rises to my cheeks as the two of them look at me.

I can't read their faces, but since when have I been any good at that? They just stand there, wet hair dripping on the towels they've wrapped around their necks, eyes on me and Sierra, who's still lying flat on her back.

"Did you go for a swim?" I quickly ask, as if that isn't obvious.

They both nod at the same time, not responding verbally to my dumb question. Nobody says anything until Sierra clears her throat and announces, "I'm going to take a quick shower." She gets out of her bunk bed, skipping the last two steps of the ladder and instead making a tiny jump. The sound of her feet landing on the floor finally bursts through my bubble. For a second I consider following Sierra's example but decide against it for the fantastic reason that leaving her bed would draw attention to the fact that it is not my bed I'm sitting on right now.

As if Sloane and Veronica don't already know that.

The moment the door to the bathroom closes behind Sierra, Sloane turns to me with wide, eager eyes. "Listen, Ellie. We need to debrief. Right. Now."

My heart stops for a second, then continues beating way too fast. My being in Sierra's bed really isn't *that* weird, right? And even if it were, there's a 99 percent chance she can still hear us talking through the thin walls *and* the sound of the shower, so can't this "debrief" wait just a little longer?

I shift on Sierra's bed as I anxiously wait for Sloane to continue, but then my muscles relax when she elaborates, "There are some groundbreaking updates regarding the Liam-and-Veronica situation."

Veronica rolls her eyes at that as I try not to sigh in relief. "I'm right here, you know," she says, and then she sits down on her bed, seemingly not caring that she's making her own sheets wet by doing so.

I look between the two teammates, my eyes switching from Veronica to Sloane to Veronica. "What's going on?" I ask, eventually settling on holding eye contact with Sloane.

"Okay, so," she starts her ramble, "a few of us were swimming, right? It's literally so hot outside, which . . . actually, you know that already. But the point is that Veronica didn't want to join us in the water, and then *Liam*, of all people, convinced her to jump in." A smile has started to creep up her face, and her eyes almost seem to ask me, *Can you believe it?*, which I definitely can't.

I look back to Veronica, intrigued. Of course I hoped the two of them would fix things, but this is way beyond my expectations. "What happened there?" I ask.

She groans, getting back up and starting to walk through our small room. As she paces, Veronica explains, "He apologized for being an asshole, and ever since, we've just been ranting together about the people we hate back home." She shrugs. "Simple as that."

"Ah," I say as the puzzle pieces fall right into place. "Of course."

She stops her pacing to look at me. "Now what's *that* supposed to mean?"

This time, I'm the one who shrugs. "Just that bonding through hatred makes a lot of sense for the two of you," I explain.

Sloane nods, the shock washing right off her face. "Yeah. Now that I think of it, Veronica and Liam might have been destined to become grumpy kindred spirits from the start."

"Soulmates," I add, and the two of us start laughing. We

laugh at our jokes until my jaw hurts and we don't exactly know if the jokes are really what we're laughing at anymore. It doesn't matter. Nothing matters except this feeling: a pure, uncomplicated kind of joy. But then the sound gets muffled by the pillows that suddenly hit our faces.

"That was *smooth*," Sloane gasps as she looks at Veronica, who I didn't even notice had picked up pillows to throw at us. "Very impressive," she adds, and Veronica smirks.

"I try."

"In all seriousness, though," Sloane says, even though she's still laughing a bit, "I'm really glad you and Liam fixed things. I guess our friend group is finally complete now that you guys are friends, too."

And even though I get what Sloane means by this, I can't help but correct her. "Almost," I tell her, and I can see her smile at me right before my gaze wanders to the closed bathroom door. "We're almost complete."

# 10. It Turns Out Ice Cream Might Not Help with Everything

On the tenth evening of summer camp, I manage to do the impossible: convince Sierra to sit at the dinner table with the rest of us. Sure, I'm pretty much dragging her along with me, but there is little resistance apart from a confused "What do you think you're doing?"

"We're friends now, remember?" I tell her. Casually. As if I didn't spend half of last night grinning like an idiot because I've actually officially befriended Sierra Levine. I settle down in my usual chair, then give her hand a tug. She gets the hint and sits down in the spot next to me. "Friends hang out together and force each other to befriend their other friends."

"I don't think that's—" Sierra starts, but I cut her off, grinning. "*I'm* the teacher this time, Levine."

She rolls her eyes at me. "It might surprise you, but I used to have a best friend, so I'm not completely lost when it comes to the world of friendship," she counters, but before I get to ask her anything about this supposed ex–best friend of hers, Noah sits down across from us, closely followed by the others, including Liam and Veronica.

"Welcome to the group, Levine," my brother says, smiling as he crosses his arms over his chest. He doesn't seem too surprised by this turn of events. He leans forward a little, then asks, "Tell me: What are your intentions with my little sister?"

I widen my eyes at him in a warning. "We were born at the same time, Noah." I sigh, then turn to Sierra. "You can honestly just ignore him."

"Hey," Noah says, holding his hands up in defense, "I'm just looking out for you. You haven't exactly had the best luck picking good friends these past few years."

I'm just about to remind him that Nina isn't as bad as he thinks when Sierra gives me a look. "Is that so?" she asks before turning back to Noah. "I just want to be in her presence."

She looks at me, and a shiver runs up my spine while heat rises to my cheeks.

"Oh wow," Noah says, echoing my exact thoughts. "That's actually a really good answer. I like her," he tells me. Then, to the whole group: "Can we keep her?"

"First off," Maya starts, "of course we will. But, second, you have to stop being extra weird. You'll scare her away before she's even truly joined our club."

Noah smiles at Sierra and me. "I have a feeling it's going to take a lot more than just my weirdness to scare her away."

And though I don't get why my brother is acting the way he is right now, I can't help but hope against everything that he's right. Because even though Daniel had a point when he said being friends with Sierra wouldn't exactly help my reputation, I want to be the sort of person who doesn't care about things like that. The sort of person who doesn't run away from something real to uphold something fake, something as artificial as reputation.

I want to be the sort of person Sierra sees in me.

From where I'm standing, I have a beautiful view of the beach, but what makes it even better is that I can peacefully watch others roll around in the sand to keep their ball up in the blue sky without having to touch either myself.

*HA! Suckers!* I think as I watch the group of people my age. Then I realize there's a really high chance they actually enjoy playing beach volleyball.

Oh well.

I turn away from the scene, joining my brother in a long line to get some ice cream. Gigi is letting us spend some time in town today, and as we probably should've expected, Noah and I aren't even close to the only ones in Bloomdale who need something to help us cool down. We've been waiting here for what feels like a very hot eternity.

"You want me to order for you?" Noah asks me when it's finally almost our turn. I nod, a flush coloring my cheeks from the heat but also out of slight embarrassment. I might be turning seventeen in less than two weeks and fully capable of ordering my own ice cream, but my social awkwardness doesn't exactly care about those facts. Since Noah is offering, I'm going to spare myself the stress.

"What kind do you want?" he follows up.

A grin magically appears on my face as I'm reminded of an inside joke we used to have with our parents ages ago.

"Surprise me," I tell him, knowing that, even after all this time, he understands those words mean he should order the same flavor I have always wanted: strawberry.

Noah's lips tug upward, his smile growing and growing and growing until he's so visibly happy, it almost makes me want to cry. It only took me saying one simple thing to get him to smile like this, which just solidifies the fact that I've caused him so much hurt by shutting him out.

My grin fades away. Before I get to say anything, Noah turns to the employee behind the counter and orders my ice cream as well as some triple-berry frozen yogurt for himself. A few seconds later, he pays, then hands me my cone.

There's no room at any of the colorful tables around us, so the two of us end up enjoying our treats as we walk around without a clear destination in mind.

"I'm sorry," I blurt out.

Noah tilts his head to the side, studying me for a moment. "Can you maybe clarify what you're sorry for? Because if you think you stepped on my toes or something, then you probably tripped over your own feet." He grins.

I shake my head and take a deep breath. "Just . . . everything these past three years, I guess." The words have barely left my mouth before I tense, quickly adding, "Not 'I guess'! That's a terrible way to apologize, I'm so—"

"Your apology has already been accepted, Ellie. No worries," Noah interrupts softly. The right corner of his mouth is ticked upward into a small smile. He puts a spoonful of frozen yogurt in his mouth before continuing. "I'm honestly just glad to see you happy again. And to finally have you back in my life for real."

"It's good"—I pause mid-sentence to lick my ice cream—"to be back."

I know there's never a perfect time to discuss things like this, but *seriously, Eleanore? You decided to do this while eating ice cream?*

"I should apologize, too, though," Noah says, sighing. I frown, urging him to go on. "My intentions might've been good, but that isn't an excuse for how much I pushed you when I found out about your list," he explains. "I knew my comments about Nina were making you uncomfortable and sad, and though that was the last thing I wanted, I just . . . kept going. I thought I was helping you in the long run, but instead I ended up treating you like something I should fix, and I'm really, really sorry for that. I didn't handle any of it well."

"Oh," I say. I didn't even know I wanted an apology for that, but it feels good to hear one. Noah's acknowledgment that what he did caused me loads of extra anxiety and meltdowns I didn't need is . . . validating. After years of being told that my feelings and I are dramatic, these words are refreshing, taking yet another weight off my shoulders.

"Thank you, Noah."

He gives me a smile. I return it, and so we walk just like that, shoulder to shoulder, until we've both finished the last bits of our ice cream.

That's when we finally find an empty bench to settle down on—one with a perfect view of the beach. We watch many seagulls fly above, listening to them squawk as we ourselves stay quiet until, out of nowhere, my brother turns to me and asks, "Do you remember when you were hyperfixating on musicals and we tried to book tickets to see one in New York City? Behind Mom and Dad's backs? When we were, like, *ten*?"

It's certainly random, but I do remember. Vividly.

A sudden laugh escapes me at the memory, one loud enough that a few people who are walking by turn around to see what's going on. A month ago, this would've most definitely embarrassed me, but now? I don't care that much, so instead of shrinking, I let myself take up some space. As I've been learning, I'm allowed to.

Noah and I sit there, side by side, him with a big grin on his face and me playfully swatting his shoulder a ridiculous number of times. We talk about everything and nothing like we used to, bringing back memory after memory until Noah gets up and asks, "You know what else I've missed, though?"

I shake my head, a little smile still lingering on my face from our last conversation topic. "Tell me."

He doesn't open his mouth; instead he shows me the answer by pulling me into his arms. Without having to think about it, I hug him back, my arms wrapped around him as I lean in.

We hug and he's sweaty and I'm sweaty and nothing about this is ideal for a hot day like this one, but that doesn't make the moment any less perfect. All that matters is that I have my brother back.

We stay like that for a while, heart to heart. Then: "Does this mean you're going to let me into your life again? For real?" His voice is muffled by my hair, and he's so hesitant. Careful. As if he's scared I'll pull away again any second now—literally.

Instead I bury my head deeper into his shoulder. "Yes," I promise.

# 11. Always Apply Sunscreen, Children

My lungs are aching and I'm gasping for air, but for once, it's not because of running too many laps.

"It's not funny!" Noah protests for the second or third time, though he's failing to hold back a laugh of his own. For the past fifteen minutes, we've been playing a game of keep-away—passing a ball among seven of us and trying to make sure it doesn't end up in the hands of the eighth person who's standing in the middle of our circle and desperately trying to catch it.

That eighth person just so happens to be Noah, like, half the time.

Yasmeen throws to Liam again, and in an attempt to get to the ball first, my brother jumps, hands frantically trying to catch it, but he ultimately fails when Liam secures it instead.

"I'm sorry, but," Liam wheezes out as soon as they've caught it, doubling over in a way that's extra funny since they're the tallest of our group, "you just look a bit pathetic standing there . . . AGAIN!" He pretty much screams then, laughing even louder than before. Unfortunately for Noah, the sound is so contagious that the rest of us can't help but join Liam once again.

We've been laughing for five minutes now, and my inability to stop has left me with a lack of balance. None of this is necessarily *that* funny, let's face it, but being in this moment, the giggles just keep coming. Every time I think I'm starting to run out, someone else says something and I'm right back to where I started, bursting into laughter again and again.

"Yeah, yeah." Noah sighs once we become a little less hysterical. "We get it. I suck at this game, and you all enjoy my misery. Why am I always the laughingstock of this group?"

Maya doesn't miss a beat, asking him, "Noah, sweetie, have you ever been part of a group where you weren't the laughingstock?"

"Touché," he admits.

"We can stop if you want to, though," Sloane assures him, but Noah shakes his head.

"No need. As long as I get to make you all laugh, I'm happy, too."

Sloane practically melts on the spot, hearts in her eyes as she looks at my brother, but it's Maya who responds. "You're such a sap."

We play for a little longer, talking and laughing until the only person who hasn't had to stand in the middle is Sierra.

"Damn, how are you so good at this?" Yasmeen asks her when Sierra intercepts the ball yet again.

Sierra shrugs. "That's what happens when you grow up with

a father who has to be playing some kind of game all the time. You get good at them."

"Sometimes," Liam says, "I forget your father is the same Adrian Levine I looked up to when I was younger."

"Honestly? Same." Sierra sighs.

Before she can elaborate, someone behind me says, "Hi, everyone!"

I spin around, coming face to face with Gigi, who is taking in all eight of us. "This," she starts, "is perhaps the strangest combination of people I've ever seen." She pauses for a second. "I like it. You have a very *Breakfast Club*–core thing going on here."

Maya gasps. "Gigi, you absolute genius!" they exclaim. "Now we finally have a club name!"

Gigi laughs at the groan Veronica lets out just as Liam protests, "We really don't need a club name, Maya."

"Yeah," Noah agrees. "Our group is already called SMASHERS!"

They proceed to get into a discussion, at which our camp counselor shakes her head fondly. Then she asks, "Ellie, can I steal you away for a second?"

Immediately my eyes search for Sierra's, trying to see if she's okay with me leaving her here. She's certainly been bonding with the rest of the group, but it's also only been, like, twenty-four hours since she joined, and I don't want her to feel awkward and alone. As if she knows exactly what I'm looking for, Sierra nods for me to go ahead.

I turn back to Gigi. "Yeah, sure."

She leads us to her cabin, where we sit down the same way

we did on the second day of camp. It makes me feel weirdly nostalgic. I'd almost want to say that version of me was so clueless, even though it was just a little over a week ago.

"How are you doing? Not too overwhelmed?" Gigi asks.

I think about it for a moment. "It is overwhelming sometimes—well, most of the time—but surprisingly, I'm surviving." I pause for a second, then add, "I guess you were right about me finding my place here soon enough."

She practically glows at my words. "I never once doubted that, but it's still amazing to hear you're doing well! Does there happen to be anything else I was right about?" Her eyes spark as her warm smile turns into a mischievous grin.

I look down at my hands, which are resting in my lap. "Yes," I tell her, knowing what she's getting at. "Apparently Sierra and I really do make a good team. I think . . . I think I really needed someone like her in my life."

"I know," Gigi says, a bit more serious now. "But make sure you don't forget that you're doing just as much for her as she is doing for you."

I think about those words. About how they might hold a truth I haven't considered yet: I could mean something to Sierra, too. Because, until I practically forced her to be my friend, she closed herself off from everyone. She wasn't here for the fun part of summer camp—she admitted that on our second day—but then I showed her that she's allowed to live a little, and now she's with our friends, playing a silly little game outside.

So yeah. Maybe I'm helping her, too.

"Gigi, what even are you? My personal angel?" I ask, at which she immediately shakes her head.

"Nope. You should actually thank David for all this."

Despite myself, I cringe at the thought of the fifty-year-old camp counselor being my guardian angel. "Oh god, now I'm picturing him in an angel costume."

Gigi decides to ignore that comment, probably not wanting to traumatize herself by thinking about it too much. A wise choice.

"Don't tell David I said any of this," she starts, "but . . . he's actually the one who came up with the idea to match you with Sierra. Which is funny, because he has *never* made a match before," she explains. "I guess he made an exception this year. He's known Sierra for a long time because of her dad. The two of them are old teammates and friends, so he's practically watched her grow up, and he knows she hasn't really been open to making any friends since her mother's death and the drama with her ex-teammates.

"When David saw you during charades, he told us you seemed like a kind, patient, and persistent person. Exactly what Sierra needed—someone who would not give up on befriending her. So there's that," she finishes. "Although David does insist the only reason he did this was to strengthen Sierra's volleyball skills. He keeps saying that a strong emotional connection between teammates makes for better players." Gigi rolls her eyes. "It's definitely true, but there's no way that's the only reason. Not that the grumpy old man will ever admit it, though. The matchmaking was always Mara's thing—Sierra's mother. She was a therapist, you know, and even though Adrian and David used to claim it was some type of emotional bullshit, at some point they couldn't keep denying that it worked."

I nod, trying to process what she's telling me. I've been wondering why a seemingly unsentimental man like Adrian Levine would care for matchmaking based on emotional compatibility, but now it all makes sense. Still, that is not the part my brain is stuck on.

*Exactly what Sierra needed,* the voice in my head repeats over and over again. The rest of Gigi's words are not nearly as interesting as that phrase. I blush for no apparent reason.

"I'm glad Sierra has David looking out for her here," I say, not knowing what else to tell Gigi.

She laughs softly at my awkwardness. "Sorry, I really was planning to just check up on you and not give you a whole lecture on Sierra's life. I'm just glad to see you two so happy. You both deserve it," she says then, leaning back in her chair. "You can go have fun now, Ellie. I'll be here whenever you need me, okay?"

I nod, forcing a smile through the sadness of my discovery. "Okay. Thank you, Gigi. All this . . . it means more to me than you know. I'm glad *I* have *you* looking out for me here."

"Oh my god," Gigi says. "With all the love in the world, Ellie, please get out of my cabin. I do *not* want you to see me cry."

I throw my head back in a laugh, opening the door. "I'll see you at dinner."

With the sun shining right on my face and the soft sound of

laughter in the background, I walk back to the spot where I left my friends behind. They're still there, playing the same game. This time, they're trying to keep the ball out of Veronica's hands, who, as to be expected, curses all of them whenever she isn't able to catch it. She even calls Liam an asshole for teasing her, which makes him laugh.

I watch my friends, not announcing my presence just yet. It's strange. A week or so ago, I wasn't close to any of these people—didn't even know some of them existed—but now I can't imagine a life in which my heart doesn't tug me toward them.

After all these years of longing for it, I think I finally know what belonging somewhere feels like. It's knowing that even when things aren't perfect, everything has fallen right into place. It's realizing that despite and because of everything, you wouldn't change a single piece of the puzzle. Not really.

I don't know how long I stand there, unnoticed, but eventually Sierra's eyes find mine. She smiles, looking at me in a way that makes me feel like there's a warm campfire in my chest in place of my heart.

"Are you going to join us or just stand there smiling like a total goof?" Sierra asks.

Without needing to think about it, I run up to the group and rejoin the game, but that goofy smile? It stays on my face for a little longer. I know that when it fades, it'll come right back, returning to and leaving me like the ebb and flow of the sea.

That evening, when we're back in our cabin and Sierra is changing out of her volleyball shirt and into her pajama top, I catch a glimpse of her back, which is almost completely red.

I don't mean to look at her while she's in just her sports bra. I really, really don't, but she just sort of . . . catches my eye.

Sierra is already putting on her top when I clear my throat and say, "Oh god, Sierra, you've seriously burned your back. Please tell me you're not one of those people who think putting on sunscreen is too much of an effort . . ."

She blinks at me a few times, but she doesn't deny the fact that she has a sunburn. Which means it must hurt, because as far as I know, she hasn't looked in a mirror yet. "I can't exactly apply sunscreen to my back, Eleanore. My arms are long but not *that* long," she explains.

I put down one of the romance novels I brought with me. It's addictive, and I really want to keep reading as I'm nearing the end, but this is more important, so I get out of my bunk bed. Sierra watches me, a frown between her brows when I disappear into the bathroom.

"I packed after-sun lotion somewhere," I let her know while I dig through my stuff. When I've found the right tube, I walk back to Sierra. "With sunburns like yours, it's best to apply this as soon as possible. I'll help."

"Oh," she says. "No, thank you."

Now it's my turn to frown. "It's really no effort. Genuinely. And I've got more than enough of it with me, so don't you worry."

"I just don't think it's necessary."

I shrug. "Better safe than sorry, right? Come on," I say, nodding toward the bathroom door. "It'll only take a minute."

Still she shakes her head. "It doesn't even hurt that—"

"Sierra, everyone and their mom can tell that protesting won't help when it comes to this," Veronica interrupts suddenly, and I'm reminded of the fact that she and Sloane are just behind us.

I look at Veronica. "Thank you!" I exclaim, even though I'm not entirely sure I should actually take her words as a compliment. But at least they make Sierra finally give in.

"Fine." She sighs, gesturing for me to go to the bathroom, "After you, Eleanore."

"You're such a gentlewoman." I smile over my shoulder, entering the bathroom.

Sierra follows me, shutting the door behind us as I open up the tube of lotion.

We're on opposite sides of the bathroom, and yet we're standing so close to each other that it gets harder for me to breathe. I take a tug of air, pushing away my sudden claustrophobia and telling Sierra to "Turn around, please. And take your T-shirt off."

I blush at the bold words leaving my mouth, but luckily Sierra immediately follows my instructions before she could've seen my reaction. Now that she's in just her sports bra, I'm able to catch more than just a glimpse of her back, and when I say her normally white skin is red, I mean it's *red*. Not a little undertone, but *actually red*.

I swallow, putting some of the after-sun lotion on my hand,

then carefully applying it to her shoulder blades. She breathes in sharply at the cold touch against her skin. Meanwhile her warm body makes my fingertips grow hotter by the second. I rub her back in slow circles, tracing the freckles on her bare skin until the thin layer of lotion is spread all over.

I pull away, trying my best not to think about the way a shiver goes through her whole body or about how fast my heart is beating right now. But everyone knows that if you desperately try to avoid thinking about something, your brain will automatically lead every single one of your thoughts back to the forbidden topic.

"There you go," I tell Sierra now that I'm done, my voice barely above a whisper.

Sierra immediately puts her T-shirt back on, then turns around so she's facing me. I used to be one of the tallest girls back in elementary school, but now I'm only just on the higher end of the average height for girls my age. Sierra, however, is as tall as you'd expect from the daughter of a beach volleyball legend. Of course, I already knew this, but only right now, as I tilt my head up the slightest bit to meet her eyes, do I acknowledge it.

For some reason, it makes my heart beat even faster. Worryingly so.

*What is this feeling?*

I wrap my arms around myself in an attempt not to shiver in the same way she just did, but I fail. Thankfully Sierra doesn't seem to pay attention to it, just giving me a nod instead. "Thank you, Ellie," she says.

"Anytime."

She turns away from me to leave the bathroom, but I grab her wrist before she has the chance. If only for an excuse to make this moment last longer . . . and to pull her closer.

She stares at my hand wrapped around hers but doesn't back away.

I swallow again. "Actually, we won't need to use after-sun lotion anymore. Because from now on, I'm going to apply sunscreen to your back every single morning. Okay?"

Sierra groans in protest, freeing herself from my grip. She leaves the bathroom as quickly as possible then, but we both know there's no escaping this.

It's like David, Gigi, and now Veronica have implied: I'm nothing if not persistent. Especially when it comes to Sierra Levine.

# 12. You Never Really Know Someone Until You Go Bowling Together

For someone who seems so intent on not revealing what tonight's surprise activity is, Gigi sure is being the least subtle person in the world.

"I can't tell you what we're going to do yet, but let's just say it's fun to do in your *spare* time. I think it will be right up your *alley*," she says, heavily emphasizing the bowling puns in her sentences. The twelve of us figured out what we were going to do before we even got on this bus, but we've silently agreed we cannot let Gigi know. Still, that doesn't make it easy to keep ourselves from laughing. Even Sierra, who has a lot of experience hiding her smiles, is almost at her breaking point right now.

Luckily, we arrive at our destination only a minute later. We all get off the bus, looking at the building in front of us. According to the huge lit-up sign, it is indeed a bowling alley.

Gigi scans our faces expectantly. "So?" she asks.

"I haven't gone bowling in *ages*," I tell her, watching as her grin widens at the genuine enthusiasm in my voice. I might not be surprised, but that doesn't mean I'm not excited.

"Yeah, this is going to be epic, Gigi," Maya says, with which Sloane and Yasmeen immediately agree.

"I never in a million years would've guessed this is what we'd be doing tonight," Sierra tries as well, but her voice comes out so monotone that I have to intervene.

I pinch her elbow, leaning in closer to whisper, "Please never try to lie again. Your acting is horrible."

"Wow, thanks for making me feel so incredibly appreciated, Eleanore," she whispers right back, her voice possibly becoming even flatter.

I laugh, putting my arm around her instinctively and dragging her into the building with me. There, an employee quickly leads all of us to one big table as well as three separate bowling lanes since, as she explains, we can't play with thirteen people at once. I end up having to play against Sierra, Maya, and Yasmeen, while Liam, Noah, Sloane, and Veronica take the lane next to us. Gigi joins the other four in the last lane.

It takes me a few turns to really get into the bowling thing, but after a couple of wasted throws, I manage to actually hit some of the pins. At least occasionally.

Yeah, no, I'm definitely losing this game.

But that doesn't really matter because, in between turns, we all sit at the big table and drink and chat and laugh. There are almost always three to five completely different conversations happening at the same time, but it's a good kind of chaos.

Even though some of the stuff that's being said is, well, *weird as hell.*

"I'm just saying, there's something very sexy about him!" Maya exclaims a little too loudly. Several heads turn our way, but it's Yasmeen whose eyes are widest.

"Maya, he's a *cartoon*."

"An incredibly attractive one!" Maya defends themself. "You just don't get the special bond between a lesbian and a fictional man."

"Yeah, I really don't," Yasmeen confirms, still giving them a side-eye.

"Wait," I say. "I've been wondering about how that works. Like, I always thought lesbians don't feel attracted to any kind of man?" I repeat the words I just said in my head before quickly adding, "You don't have to explain anything to me, of course! I guess I'm just . . . curious."

"You're totally fine," Maya assures me. "I love rambling about stuff like this. So," they start, "a lot of lesbians struggle to accept or realize that they are not attracted to men, since society wants us to believe we're straight. Eventually the belief that being heterosexual is natural gets so deeply rooted in our thinking that our brains will try to convince us we are, in fact, attracted to men. Because we think we are *supposed* to be centering men in our lives.

"Being attracted to fictional men is a way for us to tell ourselves we can't be lesbians because we like *them*, right? But they're unattainable crushes, fake feelings we can never actually pursue. This can also include celebrities and people who you think will never like you back in a romantic way. Hell, a lesbian can even date a guy and convince themself it's love when it really isn't—not in that way, at least."

Maya takes a deep breath. "So basically, even this raging lesbian"—they point at themself—"used to trick themself into thinking they got butterflies because of men. I still joke about having crushes on fictional men sometimes, actually, but no matter what, that could never truly be attraction or romantic love for me. I can make it seem like it, sure, but in the end it's simply a trick of my brain. Not to give you a whole class on my personal view of lesbianism, though," they finish with a laugh.

I blink at them. "Oh wow" are the sounds that leave my mouth eventually. "I didn't know about any of that. Being a lesbian sounds . . . hard." They laugh, but then I can't help but ask, "So do you actually get butterflies now? Like, around Yasmeen? Because I always thought that was one of those unrealistic romance tropes."

Maya smiles at me, all soft as they search for Yasmeen's hand. "When you're really in love with someone, you'll know exactly why people describe it as falling."

I go silent as I think about my relationship with Daniel. I don't know what I felt around him, but it sure wasn't anything like what Maya is describing. A part of me is still trying to convince myself it's just because it wasn't love *yet*, because I didn't allow myself to fall for him, but another, deeper part of me wonders if I'm just lying to myself.

If I could ever like him at all, even just as a person.

*But I don't have a choice, right?*

I'm still trying to answer that question when Yasmeen manages to throw a strike. Once again.

"Bitch!" Maya gasps as their girlfriend returns to the table, quite the contrast to their softness from only moments ago. "Is there anything you're not good at?"

"Plenty of stuff," Yasmeen says, sitting back down and putting her arm around them. "For example, I can never seem to get you to shut up."

Maya escapes from the hug and swats Yasmeen's arm while Sierra and I laugh, but I bet Maya is hiding a smile of their own. "You're so rude. Now I *have* to beat you," they say simply, after which it's their turn and they manage to not hit a single bowling pin.

Of course, we all howl with laughter, earning us an eye roll from them as well as, after being stubborn for a few more seconds, a loud laugh.

We talk and talk and talk, jumping from one topic of conversation to another, until we eventually somehow end up deciding to tell each other fun facts about ourselves.

"A fun fact about me," Sloane starts, looking around the table slowly, "is that I'm basically bi-cubed." Before any of us form the words to ask what that even means, she exclaims proudly, "I'm bisexual, bipolar, and a bitch!"

It takes a few more seconds before the joke actually lands with me, but once it does, laughter bubbles up in my belly again. "You're, like, the least bitchy person I've ever met," I tell her.

"Oh, just you wait." Sloane grins. "Now, why don't *you* tell us a fun fact about yourself, Ellie?"

I take a deep breath. Immediately I know what I'm going to say. "My fun fact is that, for three whole years, I strictly followed a list of seven rules . . ."

One moment, the conversation is still lighthearted, but when I start to actually recite the rules to explain how ridiculous they are, the smiles slowly fall from everyone's faces.

"Oh, Ellie . . ." Sloane says, taking my hand in hers. "I am *so* sorry people made you feel like you needed to do that."

I blink my emotions away, and then, suddenly, a little laugh escapes me. "It's okay! Genuine question, though: How did we even get here? We were laughing just moments ago!"

My brother, who sat down while I was explaining my rules, sees right through my bullshit, of course. "Don't change the subject now," he says, giving me a serious look. "I've told you this before, but, honestly, I'll keep saying it until you believe it: You are *not* too much, and people need to stop expecting you to change and instead learn to adjust themselves sometimes, too. It's like . . . humans should be treated like the sun, in a way," he tells us all.

I frown. "Um, yeah, you're going to have to elaborate there."

"When the sun is shining, nobody tells it to shine less brightly, right? We just squint our eyes and adjust. That's what people should do with others more, too."

It's silent for a good second as I process his metaphor, but then Veronica asks, "I get what you're trying to say, but what if it's a really hot day?"

"Yeah!" Maya continues, clearly just teasing Noah. "And what about climate change, Mr. Young?"

"Simply being a human doesn't cause climate—actually," he interrupts himself, "I'm not finishing that sentence. But you all know that's beside the point I'm trying to make." He looks at me again. "Nobody has the right to make you feel like you have to become smaller. You have as much right to take up space as everyone else."

I've always known Noah thinks of it like that, but even after the countless TED Talks he's given me, his words have never really come through. At least, not until right now.

For the first time, I don't look at how I've been treated as a given thing, something that just happens to autistic people. I see it for what it really is: unfair.

Cruel.

Something I am allowed to be mad about.

Pressure builds behind my eyes, like water wanting to break through a dam, and for a moment I think that this is it. This is the day I will finally cry again, but then I blink once and it's gone.

The sadness and newfound anger, however, linger.

For the rest of the night, we keep playing and talking and laughing and sharing the deepest parts of ourselves that we'd kept buried until now. Liam unpacks his own experiences with bullying; Veronica tells us about how, when she still hung out with the "popular girls" at her school, they always pressured her to date people; and Sloane shares some more about what happened last summer.

The stories keep coming and coming and coming until everyone at the table is drunk on emotions. Yasmeen is silently crying, even.

"Sorry," she says, her voice choked. "I don't even know why I'm crying anymore."

"That's okay," Liam assures her. "There's nothing wrong with being emotional, you know. And summer camp is always so intense, so it was only a matter of time before we all became emotional wrecks." They give her a smile. "I *did* warn you about the trauma dump on the first day, though."

She laughs at that, and despite the tears rolling down her cheeks, it's a happy sound.

"He's right," Noah says. "This happens every single year. We're having fun and then, boom—toward the end of camp, everyone's trauma dumping."

"What's your story, then?" Veronica asks him. "You haven't revealed any dark parts hiding behind your golden retriever facade yet."

My brother's lips part before he presses them together again, seemingly searching for the right words. Eventually he says, "I've had a pretty easy life, in all honesty."

Veronica blinks at him once, twice, thrice. "Are you being sarcastic . . . ?"

Now Noah is the one to frown. "No, I'm serious. Why do you sound surprised?" He turns to Liam. "Why does she sound surprised?"

His best friend gives him a look. "Noah, honey, you must know you don't exactly give off mentally stable energy."

"That's not a bad thing, though. You were definitely written by a woman," Sloane agrees, nodding as she puts down the can of Coke she was drinking from.

Noah tilts his head to the side. "Now what is *that* supposed to mean?"

"It's a compliment. Just take it," she tells him, a blush coloring her cheeks.

I look around the table, scanning the faces and feeling my heart warm. Eventually I get to the girl who's been sitting next to me, and I full-on grin.

"Oh no," she says as she notices the look on my face. "What are you planning?"

"Don't be dramatic." I roll my eyes. "I was just thinking that, if Noah doesn't have anything to share, then I guess it's your turn to unpack some of your emotional baggage, Sierra."

Our friends' heads whip in her direction, looking at her curiously, but all she does is lift an eyebrow at me. "Yeah right," she says, taking a sip of her iced tea. "Good luck with trying to get me to trauma dump, because there's no way in *hell* I'm doing that."

Later that night, when we're all back in our own cabins, Sierra is on my bed with me, her head in my lap and her voice choked with emotion as she says quietly, "I thought I got over this a long time ago, to be honest. But I guess I didn't after all, huh?"

She lets out a short, humorless laugh that sounds more like a covered-up sob, and even though I can't see her in this dark room, her obvious sadness cuts right to my heart.

Veronica and Sloane went to bed pretty much as soon as we got to our cabins, which was my plan as well, but then I joked about how Sierra's competitiveness was missing today. Yasmeen won both our games during bowling, and Sierra didn't seem to be upset with herself even one little bit, which felt out of character to me given the way she's normally so hard on herself during our little beach volleyball games. So I commented on it, my nosiness getting the best of me.

"I'm only that competitive when what I'm doing affects my father's opinion of me," she revealed. "It's hard not to be when he's made absolutely everything into a competition all my life. *Sierra, if you win our bet about how this movie ends, you can pick one to watch next time*," she says, attempting to imitate her dad's voice, which is much lower than her own. "Or the classic: *Sierra, if you lose this game, you're going to have to deal with my silent treatment.* I think having consequences attached to everything I do is his way of keeping me motivated so I perform at my best, but *god,* it is so tiring. I can't even have a conversation with him without it turning into a competition to see who can provoke the other the fastest."

After that, the words just sort of kept coming. She talked about all of it: how much her dad's approval affects her, the homophobia she experienced within her last team, and the constant pressure she feels.

"Here's the thing," she whispered, her voice still even at that point. "When my teammates found out I'm a lesbian a few months ago, they didn't feel comfortable around me anymore.

They didn't want to even touch my arm for the briefest moment, and they *definitely* were not happy to be sharing a locker room and a shower with me. I'd barely gotten around to feeling comfortable with my identity before they made me feel like something disgusting. Sometimes they even refused to pass me the ball during a game, even if it meant we lost the point. I still don't get that part. I guess they were either scared of being associated with my lesbianism—we already get a lot of gay allegations for being female volleyball players—or maybe they were just *so* homophobic, they thought it was a disease they could catch or something. I don't know, but eventually it got so bad that I had no choice but to leave. According to many of the parents, I was 'ruining the team dynamic.' As if I was the one refusing to be mature." She huffed, but I could hear the mix of sadness and anger and hurt she felt.

"They were my only friends, you know. I always thought I didn't need any friends besides my teammates, but I was alone all of a sudden, and I couldn't even make my father proud anymore because I didn't have a team to play games with." She swallowed audibly. "He's barely even looked at me since, like I'm not worth his attention right now. Like I've disappointed him so badly that he's punishing me with the worst silent treatment ever. Like I've lost the most important one of his games. I just hope that if we win the competition at the end of camp, he'll let me play in a team a few towns over. If I can prove I'm serious about volleyball, he'll care about what I do again—even if it's only momentarily."

I don't know how much time passed while she kept telling and telling me things, but it doesn't matter one bit to me if it's 3:00 a.m. right now. I'm just glad she trusts me.

"That sounds like a lot," I tell her eventually, my fingers lightly going through her blond ponytail. I can't believe this girl doesn't have a headache 24/7. "I'm here for you, you know. For whatever you need or want. Is there anything you want right now?"

"I want . . ." she starts immediately, her voice tired, but then she suddenly stops talking altogether. I'm convinced she's fallen asleep in my lap for just a moment when she lifts her head back up to say, "I think we should go to bed."

"Oh," I say, trying not to notice how cold my legs are now that she's completely pulled away. "Right. Yes. Of course. If that's what you want, then we'll go to sleep."

We try to get off my bunk bed without waking either Sloane or Veronica, then go straight to the bathroom to get ready for bed.

As I'm brushing my teeth and looking into the mirror, I catch a glimpse of Sierra behind me. She reaches up to her ponytail and frees her wavy blond hair. Even though we've been sharing this cabin for almost two weeks, I've never seen her with her hair down. Not even for five seconds.

But now, she's just . . . there. And she's letting me see it.

It feels weirdly intimate.

"What's up?" Sierra asks when she catches me staring, her arms wrapped around her body protectively.

I blink a few times before finally recovering. "Nothing. Don't worry," I assure her when I've finished brushing my teeth. "It's just that . . . you're really pretty." I blush, breaking our eye contact while I search for the right words. "You're always pretty, for the record. Seriously, even when you've only been awake for five minutes"—I let out a nervous laugh—"but what I mean is . . . you're pretty with your hair down, too."

"Oh," Sierra says. She looks at me for a few more seconds, then brushes her hair quickly. "Thanks."

"You know," I continue, taking her in again. She's in her pajamas—more specifically, short gray sweats and an oversized dark blue crop top—but I still can't imagine anyone looking at her and not thinking she's beautiful. Or stunning. Or whatever. "You could easily be one of the popular girls at school, actually. You'd fit right into Nina's circle."

She tenses. "Oh. Um. I don't think I want that."

I frown at her. *That doesn't make sense.* "I thought you said you wanted to talk to Nina and get closer to—"

Sierra inhales so sharply, I can't help but stop my sentence there. "Let's just go to bed before we wake up Sloane, or worse: Veronica."

Without another word, she exits the bathroom.

She walks away from our conversation just like that. Clearly she does *not* want me to know she has a crush on Nina, and, to be honest, I wish I didn't know, too.

I quickly wipe my mouth, leave the bathroom, and climb back into my bed. "See you tomorrow," I tell Sierra, after which she wishes me a good night as well, and then I guess it's done.

This day is officially over, leaving us with only two more days to spend at summer camp.

I lie there, my eyes closed as the seconds and minutes pass by. I try to let sleep find me. I really, really do, but for some reason I can't stop thinking about the way Sierra is lying right there, only a few feet away from me.

Her presence makes me toss and turn and toss and turn until I'm so restless, I can't even will my eyes to stay closed anymore.

The room is shrouded in darkness, making it hard for me to see more than just vague shapes. Still, I have a feeling her eyes are on me.

"Sierra," I whisper, my voice soft and yet a little raspy from the late hour. "You're awake, aren't you?"

I imagine she smiles at that. A true, genuine, Sierra kind of smile, where her soft pink lips curl up only a little bit but the happiness still reaches her sparkling brown eyes.

I can picture it so vividly that I'm almost tempted to reach out and tuck a strand of blond hair behind her ear. I haven't had a chance to do that before, as her hair is constantly in a ponytail, but now? Now I could. Our bunk beds aren't that far apart, so it's entirely possible for me to—

Wait.

Why would I want to tuck her hair behind her ear?

I push the thought far away along with the picture in my head of Sierra's smiling face. In reality, I can't make out anything except for her figure, and that's only vague.

She props herself up on her elbow. "You know me well," she says, her voice quiet. Careful.

I smile at the thought. *I'm glad. I love knowing you,* I want to tell her, but instead I clear my throat and ask, "What were you thinking about?"

It's silent for a while. Then: "About what you said at the bowling alley. The rules. I just . . . I wish I'd been there for you. When you were dealing with those bullies."

Even though I know she can't see it, I make a skeptical face. "You wanted to be there for me in middle school? Nobody likes middle school kids."

"Yes. I mean, no," she says, which certainly doesn't clear anything up. "I kind of wish I'd been there through all of it, actually. I like . . . knowing you," she admits, and my breath catches. "I like you, Ellie, no rules needed."

Her words wrap around me like a warm blanket, and I let myself drown in them. Let them surround me completely.

"I like you, too, Sierra," I tell her. "But you're going to make me cry."

She laughs for a moment then, and when she's done, I want to tell her to do it again. To not stop, because the sound is becoming one of the things that brings me the most joy in life. It's probably way too sappy, but my god-knows-how-late-it-is-brain wants to say it anyway.

I don't get the chance to, because Sierra swallows. "We should really sleep now, though."

"But—"

"Go to bed, Eleanore," she says, aiming for serious, but I can hear the smile softening her voice. A part of me wants to turn on my phone's flashlight just to see it on her face, too, but I'm not that pathetic. Yet.

"All right," I tell her. "I'll be quiet starting now."

"Thank you." She lays herself back down, probably closing her eyes and ready to sleep without a single worry inside her head, but I can't help myself.

I still add, "Good night, Sierra."

She groans, turning in her bed. "You're the worst."

It's quiet for a long while after that, to the point where I think she's passed out, but minutes later, she says, " 'Night, Eleanore."

I take a deep breath as that unfamiliar feeling fills me again—completely, this time—at the sound of my name leaving her mouth. It travels from my lungs to my belly to the tips of my toes, then goes back up until it's finally reached its real destination: my heart. The feeling is light and overwhelming at once, calm and chaotic, something that makes the world stop spinning and turn faster at the same time.

It's unlike anything I've ever felt before, but I'm too tired to analyze what exactly it is I'm feeling. I imagine this is what it's like to jump and let yourself fall, though, knowing you'll land exactly where you need to be.

I'm still not sure where my place in the world will be once this summer is over, and usually that scares me. But right now, I do know one thing: If I were to jump like that in this moment, I'd land right back here, in this dark room, listening to the way Sierra Levine's breathing slows down until, finally, my own eyes fall closed, too.

# 13. Note to Self: Humans Are Better Conversation Partners Than Pieces of Paper

I know this is not what Gigi meant when she told us to take some time to relax the day before the final beach volleyball competition, but the whole reason I'm at this camp is to learn to stop people-pleasing. So, technically, I'm just doing that.

My notebook lies open before me in the sand, showing two pages full of my own handwriting, while my friends talk about taking a swim. It's time I stop letting myself be distracted by the here and now of this summer. When school starts back up, I'll thank myself for focusing on working toward the solution for my problem.

I thought that by writing down all the events of the past two weeks in chronological order, I'd feel less confused about everything that's happened. Putting my feelings on paper has always helped me see things clearer, but right now, even with all the words staring back at me, none of it is making sense.

Things have been going almost exactly as planned. I've been

able to check off four out of five items on my list fairly smoothly, and yet I'm still procrastinating on the last one.

- ☑ *Allow yourself to talk more.*
- ☑ *Don't overthink too much.*
- ☑ *Stop holding back your laughter.*
- ☑ *Learn how to get vulnerable again.*
- ☐ *Let yourself fall in love.*

There has to be something I'm missing, an actual reason I haven't been able to feel stuff around Daniel. Once I've figured out what that is, I can fix *everything.*

But that's just the thing, isn't it? I can't find a logical explanation for it, so I'm totally, horribly stuck.

I read over my own words again and again and again. I analyze them, and I search for whatever it is that is sabotaging me, but eventually, when my friends demand my attention, I'm still not any wiser than before.

"What are you *wriiitiiing*?" Sloane asks me, stretching out the final word playfully. Luckily for me, she doesn't try to read what's in my notebook, respecting my privacy.

I swallow, knowing I can't tell her the truth. As good as I have become at opening up and revealing parts of myself I hadn't felt comfortable with before, telling her about my plan to win Daniel back feels like a bit too much. Especially since it reveals that, even as I claim I'll be unapologetically myself from now on, without any rules, I'm still following another kind of plan in hopes of fitting in at school. Fitting into a box.

"I'm just brainstorming," I decide to tell Sloane. And Noah, who I notice has tuned into our conversation. "Our school has some sort of tradition to make all the seniors reintroduce themselves in a presentation, to break stereotypes or whatever. I have to give mine a few weeks into the new school year, so I figured I'd start thinking about it now."

A lie. I've been actively avoiding thinking about it. I've never been big on presentations, but one in which I have to talk about myself, in which the goal is to let people know the real me? Yeah, that's forever going to be a nightmare for me.

"Interesting," Sloane says, nodding as she thinks about it. "I honestly don't know if I love or hate that idea."

I almost tell her that I, on the contrary, *do* know how to feel about it, but then Maya interrupts by letting out a loud cheer as they run to the sea. We all watch as their body collides with the water, making them shriek from both the excitement and the impact of the waves.

"YOU GUYS AREN'T GOING TO LET ME DO THIS ALONE, ARE YOU?!" they yell our way, smile growing wider and wider as Liam, Veronica, and Sloane join one by one. Eventually Yasmeen follows, too.

"You coming as well?" Sierra asks Noah and me. To my surprise, she's also walking toward the others.

I give her a smile. "I'm good for now," I tell her.

"Same," Noah agrees, and then it's just us two left.

The rest of the group is loud and far away enough that they can't hear us, but still Noah leans into me to quietly say, "So what are you actually writing about?"

I look at him, my lips parted, but no sound comes out as I try to decide what to tell him. Eventually I cave. I hand him my notebook, the page with my checklist on it open again. "My crisis," I answer with a groan. As he reads, I tell him, "I think you already assumed I came to SMASH! with a plan because, well, I always have a plan, don't I? But either way: There are five steps to it. Four of them I've completed by breaking the rules, but for some reason I can't seem to complete the last step."

Noah considers me for a second, then asks, "Who were you hoping to fall in love with? You know you can't force something like that with just anyone, right?"

I look away, blushing. "The full plan is to fall in love with Daniel," I admit, my voice so quiet I almost think Noah hasn't been able to hear it.

But then I lift my head again, and I catch my brother looking at me like I've told him I'm trying to summon a demon with nothing but a candle that cost me a dollar. "That douchebag?" he exclaims. "Um, yeah, no wonder you're failing." He shudders dramatically at the thought of it, but then he turns serious again, suddenly wondering aloud, "Why would you even want to get back with him?"

I take a deep breath, swallowing audibly. "If the two of us get back together, people will see I'm not as boring or unlovable as he claimed I am. I don't want people to see me that way."

Noah's expression gets both angry and sad from my words. I see the two emotions fight on his face, see him soften with pity only to then clench his jaw. "I swear this goddamn notebook is cursed. I wish you'd just burn it. All it ever does is make you feel awful."

I grin. "You know, I've never seen someone feel as strongly about someone else's notebook as you do," I tease.

"Um, yeah, and I have good reason to. The fact that I've been jealous of a bunch of paper for the past few years makes me feel kind of pathetic," he explains. "I always wished you'd confide in me instead."

I fall silent for a few seconds. "I never thought about it like that," I admit quietly.

"Yeah, well." Noah forces a little smile, waving his feelings away even though we both know how much he hated it. "Doesn't matter. We're friends again now, aren't we?"

I nod. "Definitely."

He gives me a soft smile, but his shoulders slump a little as he looks me in the eye again. "I'm sorry that people at school are making you feel like you have to prove yourself to them." He pauses. Then: "I know I will never truly understand the judgment you deal with, but still. Isn't the constant pressure worse than any of that? Like, every time you're at school or with Nina—or with literally anyone else, actually—you're so careful not to make a mistake. Isn't it easier to just let yourself mess up sometimes? At least that way, you have some room to breathe."

I swallow once again. "I'm trying," I tell him truthfully. My voice is fragile, as if it's one step away from breaking. "I really, *really* am going to try not to worry about pleasing everyone at school anymore, but it's so hard. I'm used to people liking me these days, but if I change this much about myself . . . even Nina could start to hate this new version of me."

Noah sighs. "I know you consider her your best friend, but *god*, that pisses me off."

We're both quiet for a second before I decide to blurt out, against my better judgment, "She's convinced you're in love with her, you know."

"Oh, I'm aware," Noah says, groaning. "I never wanted to give her any kind of signal that I was into her, but she thinks me talking to her or even just acknowledging her existence is already a sign that I'm secretly mad about her."

"Yeah, about that," I start, turning to him curiously. "If you don't like her, why do you two talk so much during history?"

He groans once more—louder this time. "She seriously told you about that?" he asks.

"Oh yeah. *All* the details," I tell him, grinning despite how much I hated listening to Nina's rambles about him.

"Well." He sighs. "If you really must know, I talked to her so I could sort of keep up with your life. You refused to tell me anything, so I kind of kept asking her stuff. *How is Ellie doing? Did she tell you about a new romance novel she loves? Is she really happy with that jerk—I mean Daniel?*"

I cringe. "Nina and I don't really talk about . . . any of those things."

Noah looks at me, clearly not surprised by this. "I know," he confirms. "Every time I'd ask something—*anything*—about you, she wouldn't know what to say. That's the main reason I don't like her, Ellie. She doesn't show even a little bit of genuine interest in your life. She only asks you basic questions when she feels like she absolutely has to or when it fits her interests. And in the meantime she just expects you to keep on giving and giving and giving her everything she wants. One supposed misstep and she already gets frustrated with you."

He turns to me, waiting for me to deny it. I don't, because deep down I know I can't. "Yeah, that's all true, but—"

"There shouldn't be a *but*!" he interrupts a little too loudly. He pauses, then lowers his voice to say, "I admire how you always want to see the good in people, and yeah, there are worse people in this world than Nina Davis. But that's no excuse for her to make you feel this way. And you certainly don't have to let her . . ." I look away, but he keeps talking. "It's your decision at the end of the day, but I don't think it's a healthy friendship. I think some distance from her would do you good."

And despite everything, despite the guilt already settling in my stomach, I don't defend Nina. Instead I say, "I really shouldn't be talking about this stuff behind her back, though. I hate gossiping."

"It's not gossiping if you're just talking about your very real feelings caused by someone's very real actions, Ellie. You're allowed to do that," Noah tries to assure me. I stay quiet for too long, so he lets it go. "But okay, we've sidetracked." He leans forward again. "What do you want to do with Daniel? Just get back together and then . . . break up once you've proven your point to everyone?"

I shake my head. "No. I want to genuinely feel good around

him. I want to *want* to be with him." My lips part then close again before I eventually say, "Sometimes I wish things with Daniel were as easy as they are with Sierra. Like, when I'm with her, being together doesn't feel like an effort. It feels . . . natural. I don't get why."

When I look back at Noah, he, for once, looks unsure of what to say.

"What?" I ask, something close to a nervous laugh escaping.

Every single word that leaves his mouth is careful as he asks me, "Do you think that, perhaps, one of the reasons things aren't working with Daniel is because you've been looking for love in the wrong place? That maybe you are capable of having the romance you want, but just not with someone like . . . *him*?"

I frown at him. "What does that even *mean*?"

Noah sighs. "Close your eyes," he commands, looking over at me to check I'm doing as he says. Even though I'm confused, I do. "Picture yourself kissing Daniel."

My whole body tenses at the thought, just like it used to do every time the kiss was actually real.

"Now," Noah continues a few moments later, "imagine it's Sierra you're kissing."

My eyes fly open. "What the fuck, dude?"

"Just do it" is all he has to say to that. And even though I refuse to close my eyes again, I can imagine the feeling of Sierra's soft lips pressed against mine. I imagine the space between us growing smaller and smaller and smaller as we kiss, as I pull her close and lose myself in the warmth of her touch.

"So?" Noah asks, pulling me back to reality.

My breathing catches in my throat, and just like in the romance novels I read all the time, the only thing on my mind is a simple *Oh*.

Because, well, *oh*.

My hands find their way into my hair as I get up, pacing around our beach towels with wide eyes. “Oh my god! I think I like *Sierra*?!” I exclaim a little too loudly before remembering she’s right there, swimming in the sea. My eyes quickly find her, but she’s too busy listening to our friends to have overheard my revelation.

Noah studies me carefully, scanning my face for a few seconds before picking up my pen and jotting something down in my notebook. Then he hands it back to me, saying, calm as ever, “Well, I guess you’ve officially completed all the items on that checklist of yours.”

# 14. For the Love of God, Keep Your Head in the Game

Playing beach volleyball is all fun and games until you have to focus on a ball while the girl you like is standing a few feet away from you, her presence making you burn hotter than the sun. And yes, that is saying quite a lot given the fact that we're in the middle of a record-breaking heat wave.

Add in the fact I barely slept last night because of this sexuality crisis, and the result is my very own personal hell.

The only thing keeping me from falling asleep right here and now is the thought of missing Sierra's reaction if we were to win the competition. We're currently only halfway through our first game, but she's been giving me a quick high five whenever we manage to score a point, so I can't help but think about what might happen if we actually win this thing. Would she give me a hug? Wrap her arms around me and squeeze me tight without even thinking about it until, just like that, we feel our hearts beating together?

Would she feel the same butterflies I'm getting while simply imagining this?

I push the thought away. *God, I really did lose my ability to think straight, didn't I?*

The girl on the other side of the net spikes hard after her partner passes the ball to her perfectly, and I have to throw myself into the sand to make sure we don't lose this rally because I wasn't focusing. Sierra runs after my badly aimed ball and ensures it makes its way back over to me in a high arc, giving me enough time to get off the ground.

I do, and then I spike as well.

The ball spins to the other side of the court, where it eventually hits the sand. *Right* within the sidelines.

Sierra turns to me immediately, eyes wide with pride. "NICE!" she exclaims, once again giving me a high five. It's even more forceful than I am used to from her. I try not to wince at the impact. "You calculated that one *perfectly*!"

"Thanks," I say with a nervous little laugh, simply accepting the compliment. There's no point in telling her I didn't *actually* intend for the ball to land there.

Sierra serves again, and so the game continues until, eventually, we win it. I don't get the hug I was so desperately yearning for, but her face does light up with an excited smile, which honestly might even be better.

Though that hug really wouldn't have hurt, either.

"You did so great," Sierra tells me as we walk to the locker room to cool down a bit between games. The temperature is much more bearable in here, so I'm surprised to find that there's no one else hiding from the sun and its warmth right now.

I settle down on one of the benches, focusing on my

breathing as Sierra does the same on the other side of the room. We don't say anything, just enjoy the silence together. That is, until I feel that tug in my chest again. The one I've come to realize means I'm longing to be closer to Sierra.

I swallow, trying to calm my heart and get rid of this feeling. Because even if she likes me in that way—which is a big *if*—being with Sierra isn't realistic, and I have to accept that.

At the start of this summer, all I wanted was to get through my last year of high school without too many eyes on me, but now there's something else I want: Sierra. The only problem is that I know these are not two things I can have at the same time.

Being with Sierra would draw so much unwanted attention to us . . . to *me*. When I was with Daniel, nobody was surprised. The two of us—we made sense together, as everyone would say. People at school even went so far as to claim we were perfect together, complementing each other in all the right ways, but Sierra and me? I can't think of a single person who wouldn't be shocked to discover I have feelings for her—including myself.

I'm not naive enough to believe that, if I try to hide it, I will just stop liking girls. I know these feelings are real and that they're not some sort of phase I'll be able to grow out of, but high school can be especially cruel sometimes, and if I'm being totally honest with myself, I don't think I'm strong enough to handle the things people would say. Especially not when I've only just gotten the voice in my head to admit that I'm not just some ally to the queer community.

"Stop overthinking," Sierra says suddenly, breaking through my thoughts. When I open my eyes, she's walking toward me, her brown eyes studying me carefully. “Do you need a hug?” she asks. “I’m sweaty, but—”

Before she can finish that sentence, I let my heart lead me into her arms, telling myself this will be a very chill, platonic hug.

Spoiler alert: It is not. I’m enjoying how she’s everything I feel and see and smell way too much for that.

“Did you just sniff me?” Sierra asks, a laugh hidden in her words, but before I even have a second to die from embarrassment, a loud voice from outside yells, “Sierra and Ellie against Zoey and Maxine on court five, please!”

I groan in protest, but Sierra ignores me, making her way over to court 5 like she knows I’d follow her anywhere.

“Let’s win this thing,” she says.

Each game we play goes a little like this: One of us serves, our opponents return the ball to us, Sierra manages to save it, I pass it to her, and then she spikes, eventually earning us another point.

I might be a much better player than I was at the start of this summer, but Sierra and I still agreed that we should try to avoid cases in which I’d have to bring the ball to the other side of the net. She’s on a whole other level than I am, obviously, and if we want a shot at winning this, we’ve got to focus on our strengths.

It’s this strategy that has us winning game after game after game. As we near the end of the competition, I’m starting to actually get hopeful about our chances of at least ending up in the top three. Even though she tries to hide it from showing on her face, I know Sierra must feel that way, too.

Everything she wanted for this summer is so close, we can almost reach it. *Almost.*

"Sierra and Ellie against Daniel and Jacob on court one, please!"

At this announcement, Sierra is the one to groan. "I'm going to be so fucking happy when we get back home and I don't have to have anything to do with that dude anymore," she mumbles.

I don't reply to that, just make my way over to the first court instead. Because I know damn well it won't be as easy for me to get rid of Daniel Solomon.

As we play the game, I try not to pay attention to the fact that it's my ex-boyfriend on the other side of the net. I don't listen to his attempts to distract me and only look at him when it's necessary to win the game. Sierra and I are playing well, maybe even at our best, but so are our opponents, and every time we score a point, they win the next rally.

We go on and on like that, our points staying close the whole time . . . until, finally, we're nearing the end of the game. They need only one more point, while we still need three.

Daniel serves the ball, of course directing it right at me. It spins my way with such force that, when I try to guide it toward Sierra with my arms, it doesn't do what I want. She still runs after it, giving her all, but it's a lost cause.

The ball falls into the sand, and my heart drops with it as Daniel and Jacob cheer, giving each other some kind of bro hug.

*Fuck.*

"Aww, Ellie," Daniel says as he sees the disappointed expression on my face. He takes a step closer to me. "You played a good game, don't worry. But you know there was no point in getting your hopes up."

"Oh please," Sierra snaps at him, still out of breath. "We made you sweat just now. *And* we beat your asses at capture the flag."

Daniel's attention leaves me, a condescending smile finding its way onto his face as he tells Sierra, "But neither of those is what really matters to you, right, Levine?"

At the sound of his condescending tone, I can't help myself. I take a step closer to him, staring right into his eyes and saying, "At least she cares, unlike you."

It's the first time I've actually told Daniel off, and it feels . . . good. Strange, maybe a little reckless, even, but good. Seeing the shock written all over his face and erasing that smug grin of his is so satisfying, and even though he doesn't deserve any more of my or Sierra's time, I don't walk away just yet.

"Oh, dude, she's feisty," Jacob says then, smirking at Daniel. I can see Daniel wants to react, but he's still not completely recovered, so I get there first.

"You're a real prick, Daniel, but you already know that, don't you?" I ask without giving him the room to answer. For once, it's my time to talk and his time to listen. "I think that, under your whole careless facade, you're aware of how annoying and cruel you really are. The only reason people tolerate it is because we're young and you happen to be conventionally attractive. They all think your future is promising, that you're going to go far, but you know you won't, and the fact of that is killing you. You're completely aware high school and, with some luck, college will be your biggest days, because afterward your charms won't work anymore. That realization has rotted your soul, hasn't it? I suggest that, instead of making other people's lives as miserable as your future will likely be, you try to find a way to prove me wrong." I can practically feel the fire blazing in my eyes as I look at him for one last second before turning around and leaving him there, stunned.

As the anger slowly fades away, though, I can't help but concede that what Daniel said holds some truth. Even though Sierra won't admit to it right now, I know she cared about this competition most of all. The whole reason she's at camp is to prove to her father that she's serious about this, that she's actually good at volleyball, and the only way to get through to him seems to be by actually *winning.*

Something that is now no longer possible. All because I lost this for her.

*We could still end up in third place,* I tell myself as we wait for our last game to start. *We could end up in third place, and that will be enough, and everything will be* fine.

But at the end of the day, we lose that last game, too, landing us in fourth place.

"Damn, Ellie!" Noah still yells enthusiastically from the sidelines once our opponents have scored their winning point. I turn to my brother, not daring to look at the disappointment that must be written all over Sierra's face.

“You really do have a feel for playing beach volleyball! I mean, fourth place? That’s so impressive,” he says. With that goofy smile of his, he bumps his shoulder into Sierra’s. “She got those genes from me, you know.”

“I don’t . . . I don’t think that’s how it works, Noah,” I remind him, still a bit out of breath from the game.

He rolls his eyes playfully. “That’s not the point, Ellie. But okay, I just wanted to say how proud I—”

“NOAH, YOU ASSHOLE!” Liam’s voice interrupts from a few courts away. We turn to where the sound came from, and we sure aren’t the only ones. Everyone around us looks at Liam, waiting to see what could possibly be going on. “GET OVER HERE! WE HAVE TO PLAY THE FINALE!”

“Oh. The finale. Right. I almost forgot about that,” Noah says to himself. Then he shouts back at Liam, “ON MY WAY!” Before he starts actually running, though, he still shoots one last look at Sierra and me. “Cheer for me?” he asks.

“Always,” I tell him, watching as he makes his way over to Liam. My brother becomes little more than a small, uninteresting dot in the distance, but I still can’t bring myself to look away and face Sierra. Not even to ask if it’s okay for me to go watch Noah’s game.

Luckily, Sierra sees right through me and my anxiety. “Please tell me you don’t actually think I’m mad at you . . .”

My silence is enough of an answer to her.

She steps into my line of vision, grabbing me by my shoulders and making sure I see the sincerity in her brown eyes when she says, “I’m not upset.”

"Are you sure about that?" I ask, still careful.

"Oh my god, Ellie, yes, I'm sure," she reassures me. "I mean, of course it would've been nice if we did win, but honestly? I'm . . . fine with this. This summer has meant so much more to me than my father's minute of approval ever could." The left side of her mouth ticks upward a little, and it takes everything in me not to full-on stare at her lips. "Plus, four is my lucky number, you know."

I laugh, releasing some of the tension in my body. "Right. Well, I'm still sorry for ruining things for you."

She frowns. "Beach volleyball is a team sport," she reminds me. "So—what's that saying?—if we go down, we go down together."

"I think that's the most positive you've been in your entire life," I joke, earning me a smirk. I smile, too. "But you're right. Maybe the real win is the friends we made along the way."

"Oh, that's horrible," Sierra says, visibly cringing at my words. "Never say anything like that again, or I'll seriously have to end our friendship."

Heat instantly rises to my cheeks at that word.

If Sierra notices, she doesn't tease me about it. "Now, are you ready to go cheer on your brother? The finale is him and Liam against Daniel and Jacob, and I'm not going to lie, Ellie—I really want to see Daniel get his ass kicked. Again."

An unexpected laugh slips past my lips, and instinctively I wrap my arm around Sierra, tugging her in the right direction. "I wouldn't miss it for the world."

# 15. Listen to Your Gut (At Least Occasionally)

Daniel, unfortunately, does not get his ass kicked. Instead, he and Jacob win the competition and the honor of taking home two gold trophies engraved with the words BEST SMASHER! in huge block letters.

I lean into Noah, who is watching Daniel accept the trophy with a distant look in his eyes. I didn't know my brother wanted to win the competition that badly. In an attempt to comfort him, I joke, "Mom and Dad will be glad you're not bringing those atrocities home, you know."

"True," Noah snorts, then looks down at his feet. With his lips pressed together tightly, jaw clenched, and shoulders slumped, he seems almost defeated. Nothing like the ray of sunshine he usually is, whether at school or summer camp. I can believe he's disappointed that he didn't win against Daniel and Jacob, but my brother really isn't competitive enough to be *this* sad over it. Meaning . . . something else has to be up. Something he isn't telling me.

I look around for a second, then grab Noah by his elbow, dragging him away even though he protests in confusion.

"Ellie? What's going on?" he asks me the moment I release my grip on him.

We're far away enough from the group to have some privacy. "I should be asking you that question," I tell him gently. "I know I'm not that good at reading people, but clearly something is upsetting you. So tell me: What's going on?"

I can see the wheels in his head turning, trying to figure out what to say, but after a few seconds of holding eye contact with me, he looks away. "Nothing's going on," he tells me.

I feel my own shoulders slump, too. Even though he's not looking at me, I shake my head. "We both know that's not true. Listen," I try, "I might sound like a massive hypocrite right now after shutting you out for over two years, but I thought we were going to let each other in again."

"We are," he confirms.

So I ask him once more. "Then tell me. Please. What is going on?"

"God, I don't even know, Ellie!" he tells me, his resolve breaking. As tears start to leave his eyes, I pull him into my arms, shocked. I let him lean on me because it seems like he needs to but also so I can squeeze him and reassure him that, here, he's safe with me.

"I don't know what's going on with me," he confesses after a bit of silence, more quietly this time. Fragile. Unlike anything I've ever heard from him. "At camp, I honestly feel fine, but now that it's coming to an end tomorrow morning . . .

I just don't know how I'm going to get through another boring year before we can come back here." He takes a deep breath, as if gathering all the strength he needs to say, "Back home, I can have the best day, the best week, the best *year* even, in theory, but when I'm alone with my thoughts, I get this almost . . . *hollow* feeling. Like I've given everything I can possibly give, and it's so *tiring*. At least here, I don't have that. Here, I feel like I'm actually alive instead of stuck in that miserably boring town."

I pull back from our hug to look at his face, swallowing as I process his words. "How—how long have you been feeling like this?"

He smiles sadly through his tears. "I'm not sure, to be honest. It feels like it's been a forever kind of thing."

My heart sinks even further. How have I never noticed Noah was feeling this way? Even with the distance I put between us, I thought I always knew how he was doing. He smiles all the time, he jokes around at any chance he's given, and nothing ever seems to bring him down.

To me, he always seemed like a person who had his life together, someone whose life was relatively easy, but I guess it turns out we're both very good at masking our feelings.

"I'm so sorry," I tell him.

"It's fine, Ellie. I'm fine," he tries to assure me as quickly as possible, but I shake my head just as fast.

"Noah, no. We're not going to minimize this."

He looks away again. "Can we at least have this conversation another time?" he tries. "I promise I'm not trying to run from this; I just want to have a fun last night at camp that doesn't include analyzing whatever my feelings mean. Okay?"

My first thought is *Absolutely not*, but then he says, "Please, Ellie . . ." and I know I can't deny him this.

"Okay," I tell him, and he relaxes, even as I add, "but you have to tell Mom and Dad you want to see a therapist by the end of *this summer*. Deal?"

Noah nods. "Deal. Thank you, Ellie."

I keep my promise—for the rest of the night, we don't talk about it. We just enjoy our last evening together with our friends, ending the summer the same way we started it: with a campfire at the beach. The same campers and counselors from that very first night sit around the fire, chatting and laughing just like before. It's almost like I'm back to the start of this summer. Except this time, the salt air around us isn't filled with possibilities. Instead, it tastes like a million bittersweet goodbyes.

We lie on our backs, none of us able to see the others' faces as we gaze at the stars above us instead.

"I wish we didn't have to say goodbye tomorrow," Sloane whispers into the night when we seem to have run out of other things to talk about. "We could just stay here for the rest of the summer, playing games and sharing stories and just being happy together. Why does this summer even have to end, actually?"

"It doesn't," Maya says, clearly in denial, too. Then, in a whisper I only barely catch: "Not yet."

A while later, Gigi stands up to speak. "Before we all leave, I'd like to say something," she tells all the campers sitting around the campfire. I happily focus on her instead of the fact that summer is really coming to an end. But then she starts her speech with "Not to get sappy or anything . . ."

Instantly she's answered with boos from all around us. One of the other camp counselors, Sam, even begs her to "Please stop *right there*, Gigi. We're too fragile right now."

"Thanks for the encouragement, y'all," Gigi says simply, her smile only getting brighter. "As I was saying, I don't mean to be a big sap, but I have some things to say about these past two weeks." She takes a deep breath before continuing. "I've always said summer camp is the perfect opportunity to do the things you're too scared to do back home. Maybe that's the reason you came here in the first place—to escape home and its expectations for a little bit—or maybe you're really passionate about beach volleyball. Whichever it is doesn't matter, because in the end, we all have this in common: We yearn to fit somewhere. Anywhere, even."

For a second, her expression turns serious. "Some of us are more sensitive to this than others, but I genuinely believe we all change parts of ourselves in order to belong sometimes. It might be subconscious, or we might be fully aware of what we're doing. The point is," Gigi continues, "summer camp is indeed the perfect opportunity to do the things you're too afraid to do back home, like showing certain parts of yourself. I sincerely hope that these past two weeks have given you the courage to do so either way."

She scans the faces all around her, her smile falling back into place. "That said, let's enjoy our last few moments together, shall we? You're not leaving this campfire for another hour, after all! Plenty of time left to do what we do best: make some more unforgettable memories!"

I look around as people cheer, some immediately getting up to run to Gigi. They wrap their arms around her, waiting for more and more people to do so until, eventually, I find myself joining in on the massive group hug, too.

From the middle of the imperfect circle we've formed, Gigi tells us one last thing: "Thank you from the bottom of my heart for these wonderful two weeks, my sweethearts. It's been an honor to watch each and every one of you grow both on and off the court."

I almost break at her words. With every passing second, I can feel the weight of these past two weeks get heavier, but I can't give in to my emotions just yet. This night has to be perfect, after all.

Dozens of campers sit around the fire, talking and laughing and roasting marshmallows. They seem to have appeared out of thin air, just like the guitar that is now being passed around and played by various people.

I'm not paying too much attention to the music, instead trying to keep up with what my friends are talking about, but then someone starts playing a very familiar song.

The song that was playing when Daniel and I shared our first kiss.

Without thinking, I turn around, hoping my eyes won't find

who I think they'll find, but of course they do. Of course he's sitting there, looking all smug while my stomach turns and turns and turns until I'm scared I'm actually going to throw up.

*You can't,* I tell myself firmly. *Don't let him ruin your last few hours here.*

So I spin back to my friends, trying to ignore Daniel's soft voice as he starts singing. I try to focus on the story Yasmeen is telling, but I only manage to catch a few words.

"You look pale," Sierra informs me then, frowning as she takes me in. "Like, *really* pale. Even more than usual. Do you need some water?"

Reflexively, I shake my head. "I'm fine. Just a little bit lightheaded, I think," I say, sounding like I'm out of breath. Maybe I actually am. At this point, I don't know. Because Daniel is giving me *that look* as he sings our song.

The crease between Sierra's brows doesn't disappear, and she follows my gaze to where Daniel is sitting, singing that stupid song and looking over at me. "Is he doing something to upset you?" she pushes, after which she curses to herself. "Shit. I should have thrown a ball in his face while I still had the chance."

"No," I say. "Daniel didn't do anything. This just always happens when I get overwhelmed. It's the autism," I joke.

"Okay," Sierra says slowly, but she still doesn't look convinced. Then: "Be right back."

She's walking away before I find the energy to think about what she could possibly be up to. But when I do, a loud *OH NO* sounds through my head.

Because what else could she be planning to do if not to curse out Daniel?

When I turn to look where she went, though, it's Gigi who is by her side, walking up to me. "Hey," she says, the sound just a whisper. Still, it makes my head ache. Even my own breathing is making my head ache right now. "I think it's best if you take tonight off to rest."

Immediately I look at Sierra and shake my head. "That's—I can't do that. This is our last night together, and I have to enjoy every second that's—"

"Let me put it differently," Gigi interrupts, still careful. Soft. "Tonight is not going to be an enjoyable memory for you if you keep crossing your own boundaries, Ellie. Please listen to yourself and take some rest."

"But I'm fine! Really," I insist, but Gigi shakes her head.

"I know what being close to a meltdown looks *and* feels like. You can't fool me."

I try to come up with a reason to keep going—because I *have* to. My being autistic shouldn't ruin my last night here . . . but the truth is, my head feels like a storm cloud. My thoughts blow by rapidly, surrounded by a dark fog that makes it impossible to see them clearly. It's weighing on me, and all I want is to lie in bed so I don't have to carry my own far-too-heavy head anymore.

The feeling is so exhausting that I can't even find the strength to protest anymore. "Okay. I'll go."

I let Gigi take me back to cabin 4. We're quiet the whole walk there, but once she opens the door for me and tries to wish me a good night, I break. Finally, after all these years of holding them back, I let the tears that have been piling up behind my eyes roll down my cheeks.

"I don't want this to be over," I tell Gigi, feeling myself fall apart bit by bit.

"Oh, honey," Gigi says, pressing a kiss to the top of my head before I climb up the bunk bed ladder and drop onto my mattress. "You're allowed to cry because it's over, you know, but please don't forget to smile because it happened," she whispers to me, and then, before I know it, sleep finds me.

# 16. Live, Laugh, Love Like There's No Tomorrow

By the time I wake up, feeling much better, everyone else is asleep.

I almost let out a loud groan at how pathetic it is that I wasted my final moments of summer camp by sleeping, but then I realize it'll disrupt the others. I can't wake everyone else up. No matter how tempting it is to have a late-night chat to make up for the time I've lost, I don't think I can.

So I try to close my eyes again . . . but then someone else groans. Or rather, some*thing* else.

The door to cabin 4 creaks as it opens, revealing two silhouettes standing in the pale moonlight.

"Wake up," Yasmeen whispers, carefully tapping Sloane's shoulder to make sure she doesn't startle.

Maya simply turns on the lights. A bit too ruthless for my liking, but definitely effective.

"What's going on?" I ask, squeezing my eyes shut because of the bright light. "Isn't it, like, the middle of the night?"

"It's exactly twelve a.m., yes," Maya confirms a little too happily, at which Veronica lets her head fall back onto her pillow. "Don't go back to bed yet!" Maya protests, looking at us with puppy eyes even though Veronica can't see that with her head burrowed in her pillow. "It's our last night together! We have to do something fun!"

"But consider this: Sleeping *is* fun," Veronica tells them, voice muffled by the pillow. She turns around so she's lying on her back. "And besides, aren't you two supposed to be in your cabins right now? I thought we aren't allowed to leave them past ten p.m." She directs the last part at Yasmeen, likely not wanting another chaotic answer from Maya.

"Yeah, we're supposed to be sleeping, too, but this one"—she looks at Maya—"won't let me until I convince all of you to sleep under the stars with us." Yasmeen sighs. "So? What do you say?"

Sloane's tired eyes widen. "There's no way we'll get away with that. Adrian is always the first to wake up, so even if no one hears us right now, he'll find us in the morning."

"We've set an alarm for five a.m., so we'll go back to our cabins then," Yasmeen explains, clearly having thought this through. "And from what I know about Adrian, he probably wouldn't care that much even *if* he found out." She looks at Sierra then, pulling an awkward face. "No offense to your father."

Sierra snorts. "None taken. You're right, actually."

It's quiet for a second as everyone considers if this is a good idea. And maybe it isn't, but as I think about the fact that we have less than twelve hours left together, I can't help but want to make every single second count.

"I'm down," I tell them, surprising myself most of all.

"Same," says Sierra, and then, after a beat of hesitation, Sloane nods, too.

"Okay."

Now all eyes are on Veronica. "Ugh, *fine*," she groans, noticing our staring. "But if I don't get enough sleep, you will all have to deal with my moodiness tomorrow."

"We're quite experienced with that by now," Sloane says, grinning as Veronica glares at her.

Before we all go to the beach to sleep under the stars, Maya quickly runs back to their own cabin to grab something, and the rest of us drag Liam and Noah out of bed and grab our sleeping bags. When we reunite with Maya, they're carrying the biggest bucket full of candy I've ever seen.

Yasmeen is the most flabbergasted of us all. "Where have you been hiding that thing all this time? It's bigger than your head!" she exclaims.

But Maya just says ominously, "A magician can never reveal their tricks . . ." They grab a handful of candy and offer it to us. "Candy?" Maya asks, and that's all it takes for us to drop the mystery.

I put a gummy bear or two or three in my mouth as we walk to the beach. Once there, we all settle down in the sand with our sleeping bags, turning on the flashlights on our phones so we can at least sort of see each other's faces. In the middle of our group, the massive bucket stands.

We all grab a piece of candy, holding them in the air as if to toast. "To our last few unforgettable hours together!" Maya says, and everyone cheers, although there's a bittersweet taste to it.

Liam doesn't participate in our half-depressing cheer. Instead he lets out a frustrated groan at the reminder that we're leaving tomorrow. "Enough of this misery, please! This isn't the end!" they say, and though they try to hide it, I watch them swallow in the faint light of our phones. "We're not in the Last Supper or some other . . . *tragedy*, okay?!" he tells us, picking his phone up out of the sand and beginning to type frantically. A few moments later, my own phone buzzes, and so do those of my friends.

"We live in the twenty-first century, y'all. There's this magical thing called a group chat in which we can all talk to each other whenever we want," Liam explains. "I get that this feels like the end, but it really isn't."

It's quiet again for another second before Veronica speaks. "How the fuck did you even get my number?" she asks, looking at her phone screen.

Liam's eyes widen in panic before they cross their arms over their chest protectively. "Not right now, Veronica. Our time is ticking."

I take a deep breath, straightening my back as I say, "Liam does have a point. We should definitely keep in touch outside of camp. We *will*, but that doesn't mean I'm not going to miss all of this." I gesture to everything around us—the cabins and the counselors in the distance and even the peaceful atmosphere that's still to be found in the air between us, right here. In Bloomdale.

Sierra raises her eyebrow at me. "Are you saying you are going to miss the sand?" she asks.

"Okay, maybe not *everything*," I correct myself, a laugh almost breaking through my sadness. Almost. "Living in our little bubble together, though? Yeah, I'll miss that."

Liam looks down at his feet. "Fair enough. Same here," they admit. "But I don't want this night to turn into some goodbye already. Please, let's just enjoy it like there's no tomorrow, okay?"

So we do.

I would say sleeping under the night sky together was a great idea, but so far not a lot of sleeping has actually occurred for me.

Everyone is quiet, and to my own surprise, the ground I'm lying on isn't that hard. In theory, I could easily fall asleep here, but whenever I close my eyes, I find myself opening them again a few seconds later.

I toss and I turn and I try. I really, really, *really* do try to sleep, but there's just too much energy in my body that needs to go somewhere else first. So that's why I end up doing something I never in a million years thought I'd do: I decide to go for a walk at three in the morning.

I get up slowly, careful not to wake up any of the people lying around me. Maya does groan at some point, but since they don't say anything, I assume it's just because of something that happened in their dream.

I glance back at the group one more time, just to make sure they're asleep, and then, with nothing but my phone in my pocket and my earbuds playing music in my ears, I leave.

Thanks to the soft song that starts playing and the beautiful view above me, my heart rate finally slows down. As is to be expected at an hour like this, there's no source of light except for the full moon hanging in the sky, surrounded by dozens of stars. From where I'm standing, they're nothing more than tiny dots breaking through the darkness, yet I'm unable to take my eyes off them.

I continue walking in a straight line, completely at peace as I look up at the night sky. That is, until a hand suddenly grips my wrist.

I spin around, my heart beating out of my chest again. "Where the hell are you going?" the person holding on to me hisses, her familiar voice soothing despite her harsh tone.

"Sierra." I sigh in relief and take out an earbud. "Thank god. I really did see my life flash in front of me for a few seconds." I laugh.

I can barely see her face in the darkness, but I'm still able to make out her frown. "Where are you going?" she repeats, loosening her grip on me, but only a little bit.

I look down at my feet. "I couldn't sleep, so I thought it'd be a good idea to take a quick walk. To clear my head and get rid of some adrenaline and all that."

She doesn't say anything for a few moments. I'm already

half convinced she's decided to just silently judge me when she clears her throat. "That's a horrible idea, actually. Mind if I join?" she asks.

I blink once, twice, thrice before a smile finds its way to my face. "You know I'd never dare say no to your company."

We start walking next to each other, our footsteps syncing as we go farther and farther away from the rest of the group. "So," Sierra starts, her shoulder bumping into mine ever so slightly. My breathing catches at the realization that this is the first time Sierra and I have been truly alone since my conversation with Noah.

Since I discovered that the way I feel around her isn't exactly purely platonic.

"So," I repeat after Sierra. Then I take a deep breath. "Listen," I quickly say, "I'm sorry if I freaked you out earlier. With my meltdown and all."

Sierra shakes her head. "You literally have nothing to be sorry for," she insists. "Seriously."

"It's just . . . you didn't ask for any of that."

She raises her eyebrow at me. "Neither did you."

"But that's different. You know, since I'm the one who—"

"Ellie," she says. Her tone is so resolute that I have no choice but to believe every single word that leaves her mouth. "I mean it. I said I wanted to be there for you a week or so ago, and that doesn't just mean when you're happy or when you have something to give to me. The only person I'm upset with right now is myself."

She scans my face carefully, almost as if she's searching for something. Her eyes reach my lips, and she gulps before she meets my gaze again.

"Why are you upset with yourself?" I ask. Her lips part, then close as she blinks at me again and again. As if she can't believe I don't know the answer to my question already. "I'm autistic, Sierra," I remind her. "I'm not that good at reading between the lines."

She looks away, shaking her head and snickering a little. "Right. My bad. I guess there are a few reasons, but mostly . . . I just wish I could've helped you when you were having your meltdown. The truth is, I don't know a lot about autism." Sierra sighs. "I've been doing some research, but—"

I stop her, feeling like my heart just squeezed upon hearing her words. "You've been doing research?"

"Well. Yeah," she says, shrugging. Like it's nothing.

And maybe, in reality, it kind of is the bare minimum—the least a friend of mine can do is learn how to help me during a meltdown—but right now it feels like she's just handed me the world. Because outside of Noah and my parents, I don't think anyone has ever done that kind of thing for me.

It's kind of sad when I really think about it.

"I could literally kiss you on the mouth right now," I tell Sierra, trying to let her know I'm grateful. But then she looks away, and I freeze at how awkward that comment is.

*Great job, Eleanore.*

Except Sierra looks just as flustered by the thought as I am. She's blushing and can't seem to meet my eyes anymore, which could mean . . .

Could it mean what I hope it means?

My voice comes out more high-pitched than usual as I quickly add, "*Anyway.* Autism is a really broad spectrum, so doing research on us is a little . . . complicated sometimes. It's still good to google stuff to get a general idea of what to do, of course, but if you want to know what one specific autistic person needs, it's best to always ask them since our needs truly differ."

"So . . . what do you need?" Sierra asks, still not looking at me.

I stare in the same direction she does, thinking about it for a moment. Then: "Depends on the situation. Sometimes I need someone to hold my hand or wrap me up in their arms and whisper that they're here so I know I'm not alone. Other times, I need to lie down in a dark room all by myself."

She nods, thinking it over. "And right now?"

"I—" I pause, then decide to take the risk. It's now or never. "I want . . . you," I admit, the confession nothing more than a whisper in the night.

"Well," she says, finally meeting my eyes again, "here I am."

I don't say another word. Instead I take a step closer to her, gauging her reaction before leaning in to kiss her.

Her lips are soft against mine—just like her hands are as they find their way to my waist. I gasp at the feeling of Sierra's fingertips on my exposed skin, and she takes the opportunity to deepen the kiss, tugging me closer, closer, closer until I'm pressed against her with no room left between us.

I don't mind even a little bit.

This is everything I didn't know a kiss could be, but most of all, it's perfect. Nothing about it is like how it was with Daniel. This isn't a kiss that I simply let happen to me, not a thing I have to tell myself will be over in a few seconds. Rather, it's something I'm not sure I'll ever truly get enough of.

There are so many ways to describe this—new, exciting, fun, almost like being embraced by a thousand flames without burning—but then Sierra pulls away, putting an abrupt end to it.

"I don't know if this is a particularly good idea when it comes to getting rid of the adrenaline in your body," she says, her voice rushed and breathless.

She's right, of course, but her hands are still on my waist, and my heart is beating so fast, and it's already far too late now, so I quickly tell her, smiling, "Completely worth it." Then I press my lips against hers again.

She pulls me closer to her once more, not needing me to repeat myself at all. I can't help it. I smile into the kiss, and I keep on smiling long after it comes to an end.

Everyone is luckily still asleep when we return. The two of us settle back into our sleeping bags as quietly as we can, that smile still present on my face when she turns to me again.

"Good night, Sierra," I tell her.

"Sweet dreams, Ellie," she whispers right back, taking my hand in hers. I let her.

And I don't know if I'm drunk on sleepiness or on my proximity to Sierra, but even as I lie awake for a little longer, under a sky full of stars, I don't worry about what will come tomorrow for a single second.

# 17. As a Wise Woman Once Said: Let It Go

The moment I wake up, I'm hit by the knowledge that my time at summer camp is quickly running out, but if I had somehow managed to forget, Maya's alarm sure would've reminded me.

"Is that 'Wake Me Up Before You Go-Go'?" I ask them, barely able to keep my eyes open as the familiar song blasts through their phone.

"It sure is," Maya says, and judging by the sound of shuffling sand, they've somehow already gathered the strength to get up, even though nothing about the dark sky above us makes me want to get up. "I thought it'd be fitting. Now let's all get our asses back to our cabins before Adrian notices we're gone and kills us, or worse: before I get emotional while Wham! is playing."

Even though the thought of crying with this song on in the background feels ridiculous, it's a valid fear. We don't say it yet, but we all know what today marks: the end.

No matter what, when these last few hours are over, we're never going to get to relive this summer—not really. Sure, we'll have our memories, loads of pictures, and probably also the ability to replicate the feelings coursing through our bodies right now, but we'll never be here, living in this moment, again.

The thought terrifies me so much that for the next few hours, after we go back to sleep and are later woken by Gigi and told to pack our bags before breakfast, I can't go even a few minutes without calculating how much time I have left to enjoy being here.

Three hours, then two, then only an hour and a half.

The counting stops only when Sloane and Veronica announce they are done packing, leaving me and Sierra alone in cabin 4. As soon as the door closes behind them, time, which has been moving so quickly, stops again.

Because, *oh my god*, Sierra and I kissed last night, and I haven't said a single thing to her yet, too caught up in my own overthinking.

It's not that I regret what I did, but I can't deny that the late hours made me bolder than I usually am. Now that it's daylight again, I know I realistically can't ask her out. Not when I'm unsure if I can deal with the consequences of us being together.

Even after an entire summer of working on my confidence, of trying to make other people's opinions not matter to me, I don't think I can handle people at school targeting me again. Though I hate to admit it, Daniel had a point. Even just associating with Sierra could do damage to my carefully built reputation. I shouldn't care. I know I shouldn't, but I'm not dumb. My feelings for her go so much further than just wanting to *associate* with her, which would mean burning my reputation altogether and not letting the flames get to me.

But the truth is, I'm scared I would simply burn right with it.

No. Even if I assume Sierra feels the same way I feel, I can't date her while I'm still unsure about who I am.

Sierra deserves to know as much.

"About last night . . ." I start, quickly putting the words out there before I get cold feet. Still, I can't bring myself to look her in the eyes. "You're probably going to think I'm a selfish bitch for kissing you while I'm still figuring things out, and I wouldn't blame you for that, but I just wanted to ask if you could please not tell anyone about . . . it? This is all very new to me, and I just don't know if I can—"

"Breathe, Ellie," Sierra says then, getting up to sit down right next to me. As she's walking over to me, I wonder if she's going to kiss me again, if she knows that I'd let her, but then she stops moving once we're side by side. "I would never out you, okay? So don't even worry about that. What happens at camp stays at camp," she promises, reaching her pinkie out to me.

I link mine with hers, exhaling in relief as I say, "Deal."

And I don't know about Sierra, but in that very moment, as we sit there, just looking at each other for a few seconds, my heart is filled to the brim with warmth. All caused by one simple touch.

If we kissed right now, I think I'd explode, but for the first time in my life, I crave to be overwhelmed. Because it's worth it if it means I get to be closer to Sierra Levine.

An hour and twenty minutes later, the faces around me are the exact same ones that were here a couple of weeks ago, at the first campfire. There's only one big difference: Today I recognize all of them. I spot the person with the blue buzz cut who I played charades with on the very first day here, the guy who I talked to only briefly but who still managed to make me laugh, and the young girl who absolutely humbled me when I played volleyball with her. Each person I see brings back a new memory, a new feeling, a new story.

A new goodbye.

I hug the people who are leaving, no matter how little interaction I've had with them, until . . .

"Ellie and Noah Young, your parents have arrived!" Gigi yells through a megaphone, closely followed by Maya gasping, "NO, PLEASE, NOT NOAH AND ELLIE! TAKE ME INSTEAD!"

I almost manage to laugh because of that, but nothing about the mass of people coming to hug us is funny. I embrace what feels like a hundred people in two minutes. They keep coming, and my voice is choked with emotion as I tell each of them goodbye. Because even if we've only had a small, meaningless interaction once or twice, the fact that I'm most likely never going to see these people again hurts. It's the ending of something that never truly began, leaving me with numerous what-ifs and no tangible evidence of loss.

No broken heart, just a weird feeling that makes it beat in an unpleasant rhythm.

But then, once the hugs stop coming every three seconds, it's time to say goodbye to our close friends, and I feel the cracks start to form after all.

Everything is silent as I turn to Sierra, Sloane, Veronica, Liam, Yasmeen, and Maya. There's so much left for me to say to them, so many stories I still want to share and jokes I want to make, but nothing I come up with right now feels right for this moment. So I open up my arms for the next person to fall into, saying one simple thing.

"Come here."

As I hug Maya, then Yasmeen, then Sloane, and so on and so on, I let myself lean on each of them, knowing they won't let me fall. In response, they squeeze me tighter. When I get to the last person—Sierra—tears are streaming down my face. Just as I want to tell her goodbye like I did with the others, she whispers, "See you at school, okay?"

I can't bring myself to do anything but nod, and then it's really over. Even the goodbyes are behind us.

"We'll text," I tell my friends, and they all agree, whether silently or aloud. As Noah and I turn around and follow Gigi to our parents—each of us looking back too many times before our waving group of friends is officially out of sight—that's what I hold on to.

*We'll text, we'll text, we'll text,* I repeat in my head over and over again. *We'll text, and everything will be fine.*

But then I'm in Dad's familiar black car, listening to both my parents express how happy they are to see me and Noah again, and I break down completely. Tears quickly cover my cheeks as a sound I didn't know I was capable of making leaves me.

Noah grabs my hand, squeezing it gently while I try to breathe, a silent signal that he's here for me as Mom shoots one simple question at me, eyebrows pulled into a concerned frown: "Do you need me to make an emergency appointment with your therapist?"

I quickly shake my head. "No, I don't think that will be necessary," I say between ragged breaths. "But . . . thank you, Mom," I tell her, my tears falling quicker and quicker. "And Dad. I love you both so, so much."

Mom's eyes soften, some of her worries fading away but clearly not all of them. "We love you, too, sweetie. Are you sure you're doing okay?"

I think about that for a second. I'm crying, and my heart is beating abnormally fast, and I feel so much sadness, and yet . . .

"Yes, I think I'm okay."

She relaxes, if only for a few short seconds. Because that's when Noah clears his throat and cuts in, "Speaking of therapy, though . . ."

I immediately get what he's going to say, and this time, I squeeze his hand, hoping it comforts him even half as much as his presence comforts me. He takes a deep breath, after which he continues talking.

"I've been thinking. My life is pretty great. I have great friends, great grades, the greatest family, and I like to think I have a great future ahead of me, too, but . . . I've been struggling these past few months," he admits, voice trembling. Another inhale, then: "I don't know what's going on with me, in all honesty, but I do know I'm tired. A lot more tired than I should be. And I think it'd be a good idea if I tried out therapy, too."

Mom and Dad don't interrupt Noah as he talks, except if you count the occasional nod to let him know they're listening. There was never a single doubt in my mind that our parents would be understanding of everything, but I still feel Noah's body relax when Mom says, "Oh, honey, I'm so sorry to hear this, but thank you for telling us."

"We're here for you, son," Dad adds. "When we get home, we'll get you an appointment as soon as possible, okay? We love you."

That's when Noah breaks as well. "Thank you," he says. "I love you, too."

"But," Dad continues, straightening his back as the roads flash by, "may I now ask what in god's name happened at that camp?"

My brother looks at me, a smile on his face as he gestures for me to go ahead, and I can't help but laugh through my tears, too. "Well, it all started with a list . . ."

# 18. What Happens at Camp Stays at Camp

A week passes, and I barely hear from Sierra.

It's not like I reached out to her specifically or anything, but we've both been active in the camp group chat. Everyone's been talking nonstop in there, whether that means we've been sending each other memes or complaining about being bored or just sharing a random story of something that happened to us that day. The point is: It'd be so easy for her to just slide into my private messages.

But she hasn't.

*Why hasn't she? Is this what she meant when she told me what happens at camp stays at camp?*

"You could start a conversation with her yourself, you know," Noah tells me for the billionth time, knowing exactly what I'm so lost in thoughts about at the moment. I've told him everything, of course, and he thinks I should just shoot her a message instead of endlessly overthink it . . . but I can't. Right?

Yes, we were friends, and yes, that friendship ended with us kissing. But that doesn't immediately mean she likes me. Maybe I was just a girl she wanted to kiss at summer camp, and now that chapter is behind us.

I should just forget about it before I make things awkward for the whole group.

I pick up my phone and go to Sierra's profile. A green dot lets me know she's online right now, but when I open our empty chat and wait for the typing symbol to pop up, it never does. No *hi*, no *it's almost your birthday*, no anything. She's probably just going to send a message to the group chat like the others.

But I don't want her to be like the others. I want her to be more than that.

Before I find the guts to type something myself, my screen goes dark again.

"Sorry," I tell my brother, leaning my head on his shoulder and watching as our two birthday candles dance in front of our eyes. Somehow, even that's a reminder of Sierra and me. "Less than a minute until our seventeenth birthday and I'm still killing the vibe." I sigh.

Noah chuckles, putting his arm around me. "Believe it or not, this is the best birthday countdown I've had in years. Now," he adds, "thirty seconds left! Are you ready to make a wish?"

Despite the way I'm feeling, I nod, giving him a genuine smile. "Yes."

The two of us start counting down the seconds until midnight hits, sitting shoulder to shoulder when we blow out the candles. And as I watch the two lights go out, taking both of our wishes with them, I can't help but believe that everything will eventually feel okay again.

Because no matter what happens next, I've got my brother by my side.

# 19. Don't Do . . . Whatever the Hell Led to This

The thing about throwing a birthday party in Willowmoor is that, no matter how selective you are with your invitations, there's always going to be more people showing up than you plan for. I'd heard others claim this, but for some reason I didn't think the rule would apply to me and Noah.

But as I watch yet another group of people I've barely talked to enter, I realize I definitely thought wrong. These people aren't even trying to pretend like they're not using our birthday as an excuse to party; they simply walk past me without saying a word.

Noah told me not to pay too much attention to it, but I can't help watching the door. Constantly. Though there might be another reason for that, too.

There's still a part of me that's hopeful Sierra will show up any minute now, saving me from the misery and loneliness I'm feeling at my own party. Sure, I could talk to Noah for as long as she doesn't come, but he's busy spending time with his friends and introducing them to Sloane. Neither Noah nor

Sloane seems to have made a move yet, but it still doesn't feel right to join in on the conversation while the two of them are making heart eyes at each other.

So I stay close to the door, Nina sticking by my side like she's been doing for most of the night. In theory, she should be able to put an end to my loneliness as well, but . . . I don't know. There's something about our conversations tonight that simply isn't working for me.

She rambles on and on about this really cool concert that she went to with her older sister, Samantha, sharing every single detail with me, and I can't bring myself to care in the way I used to whenever Nina talked about her life.

I can't help but think that, maybe, it's because nowadays I'm used to something more than this. Something like how I felt around Sierra. And Veronica. And Yasmeen and Maya. Sloane, my brother, Liam.

I just want that feeling back.

When I was at camp, I thought I had fixed everything that needed to be fixed, but even though I feel like I know more about myself now, I'm stuck in my old life again. My old feelings, my old friends, my old self.

Nina is still talking on and on when the door finally opens once more. My heart rate picks up as I wait for a face to appear, all the while internally grumbling about how pathetic this is. And it is. I've been standing here for way too long now, my heart sinking every time I realize it's not Sierra who's showed up.

But this time, it doesn't. My breath catches in my throat and I blink again and again before believing my own eyes.

Because right there in the doorway is Sierra Levine. Everything about her is just the same as the last time I saw her—perfect blond ponytail and all.

I would say she lights up the room, that even in the dark I feel her shine, but Sierra is probably too grumpy to qualify for that metaphor. The sight of her does, however, light up a dark space in my heart.

And when she looks right at me, I feel my body move in her direction on its own. Like it's a reflex, something my brain doesn't even need to think about.

I almost run right to her, but Nina snaps, "Ellie? What the fuck? Are you even listening to me?" The suddenness of the sound makes me break my eye contact with Sierra, and all my muscles tense as Nina follows my line of sight. "Huh? What is *she* doing here? I've literally never seen the two of you talk to each other."

I hold myself back from saying that I haven't really spoken to half the people here right now and that a good part of the other half are people I *wish* I had never spoken to. Like Blake, for example. Or Daniel, even.

"She was at beach volleyball camp, too," I explain, hating how it makes it sound like Sierra means nothing more to me than someone who was once at the same place at the same time as me. I look down at my feet, nervously adding, "The two of us spent quite some time together, actually."

"Oh," Nina says. There's a slight frown between her brows, as if Sierra and I are an equation she can't quite solve. Then she clears her throat. "She and I used to be friends, you know. Like, *ages* ago, and only because we were neighbors who didn't have anyone else our age to talk to."

Instantly I think back to the deal I made with Sierra, about how it didn't make sense to me why she would need me to talk to Nina. At least, not until now.

If Sierra and Nina used to be close, then that must mean Nina is the ex–best friend Sierra once mentioned. Maybe they had some sort of falling-out years ago and now Sierra wants to make it up to the girl she actually has a crush on—the girl who is not me.

*God, how could I forget about her obvious crush on my best friend?*

Of course Nina and Sierra are meant to be. It's the way it was always supposed to be, which I should've known. That's how these stories go. I shouldn't have let myself get so caught up in the idea of Sierra and me when we were doomed from the start. When I'm clearly supposed to end up with Daniel.

Dread fills me to the brim until there's almost no space left in my lungs for air, but no matter how difficult it gets, I need to *breathe*. I can't let my feelings distract me any longer.

As Sierra briefly glances between me and Nina, it hits me. I never actually completed my end of the deal, so now Sierra is here to remind me of it. So I can get Nina to talk to her again and they can fall hopelessly in love.

*With each other.*

My jealous mind sighs at the thought, and finally my heart sinks again, falling down, down, down until every last trace of the hope I was still holding on to is officially gone.

Still, I swallow my pride and turn back to Nina. "Could you maybe do me a favor?" She gestures for me to go on, so I spit it out: "I need you to talk to Sierra for me. Right now."

Nina's frown deepens as she crosses her arms over her chest. "Why would I do that?"

"Just . . . go talk to her for me, okay?" I plead, knowing I'm not strong enough to explain everything. "Please?"

Nina studies me for a second, then nods, suddenly softening. "Fine. Anything for you."

*See?* I tell myself. *She* is *a good friend.*

Then Nina enters the crowd, and I watch as she walks up to Sierra. She taps her on the shoulder, says something, then leads her to the kitchen, and as I watch the door fall shut behind Sierra, a realization dawns on me.

Sierra and I are nothing to each other now. Not lovers or exes, not friends, not two people helping each other out. We don't even qualify as strangers anymore after everything that happened this summer. Just . . . nothing.

In a matter of seconds, tears press behind my eyes, and though I manage to blink them away at first, my sight slowly gets blurrier. Before I let anyone see me cry, I run up the stairs and to my bedroom. Luckily everyone is too busy partying to really notice me.

But once I open the door to my bedroom, hoping to get some alone time, I see someone else had the same thought.

"Oh my god." I gasp as a wide-eyed Noah and a blushing Sloane break their kiss—against the wall of *my* bedroom. "Dude," I start, "your room is literally five steps away."

Noah splutters for a few seconds before saying, "I didn't plan this! I just wanted to show her that old picture of the two of us that I thought was in here, but then I couldn't find it, and now we're . . . well, here."

I shake my head at him, but still I can't help the grin that slowly creeps onto my face. "It's in the middle drawer of my desk. Thank me later," I say before I go to close the door, then change my mind. "I ship this, by the way," I let the two of them know. I manage to catch a glimpse of Noah threatening to throw a pillow at me just as I close the door.

Moments later, giggles sound from behind my bedroom door, and I smile.

At least one of us gets to be happy and in love.

When I see Sierra's face again, she's pushing herself through the crowd as quickly as possible, eyes pointed at the door and nothing else. I can barely see her expression—and even if I did, I probably wouldn't be able to read it—but something about the scene sends me into panic mode.

For one simple moment, my jealousy is irrelevant. It doesn't even matter to me if she doesn't want anything to do with me anymore. I just need to know if she's okay.

The door has already fallen shut behind her, but I still attempt to get to it as fast as I can, stepping on a few people's toes in the process. For once, I don't even bother apologizing.

I've just reached the door, hopefully still with time to catch her outside, when Daniel steps in front of me.

"Ellie, hey!" he slurs, a stupid grin on his face as he looks at me. He reeks of alcohol, but the reason I flinch is mostly due to the fact that he put his hand on my shoulder. "I've been looking for you. To wish you a happy birthday and all," he tells me.

Despite myself, I give him a polite smile. "Thank you, Daniel. Can you give me a moment, though?"

Before he can reply, I run outside, looking around in a desperate attempt to find Sierra. And I do. She's only just jumped onto her bike. The light from the lampposts is making her hair golden on this dark night. I'm about to start running—I don't care that people are probably looking at me—when Daniel holds me back yet again.

This time he grabs my wrist. I look at him over my shoulder in surprise.

"Ellie," he says again. "Can we talk, please? It's really important."

I want to snap at him, want to tell him to leave me alone even though I know I shouldn't fight the inevitability of us anymore. When I look around again, Sierra is already gone. Every bit of energy leaves my body, to the point where I don't even bother fighting free from Daniel's grip.

He seems to take that as a green light to continue talking. "I've been thinking a lot this past week," he tells me, still not letting go, "and I've come to the conclusion that I'm a total dickhead." He lets out a short laugh, then turns serious again, gazing into my eyes.

*What the . . . ?*

"I know you've accepted my apology for what I said at the party already, but I need to say sorry again. Because I never should've broken up with you in the first place."

He reaches out and tucks a strand of hair behind my ear. I should lean into it, maybe, but I'm too shocked to move. "I guess what I'm trying to say right now is . . . Ellie, will you please take me back?"

I blink at him, trying to process what exactly he's telling me, but before I get to give him an answer, the worst possible thing happens.

All these messy feelings—they come right up, and I can't hold them back anymore.

So I throw up.

Right on Daniel.

People around us gasp and laugh. I hear a guy say, "I'm guessing that's a no, dude." There's even a flash as someone takes a picture. Luckily I'm already running away by then, hopefully preserving some of my dignity.

I leave Daniel standing there, confused, while I fly up the stairs and into my room. Except for the pillow on the floor, there isn't a single trace of Sloane or Noah left.

I lock the door behind me. A sob slips past my trembling lips only moments later, tears quickly falling as my heart squeezes and aches and *hurts*. Before I have to throw up again, I grab my trash can and hold on to it for dear life for the rest of the night.

I hide upstairs throughout the rest of Noah's and my party, wallowing in self-pity as I think about how I've ruined everything.

With Sierra. With all the people who saw me break down just now. Hell, even with Daniel, whose opinion I shouldn't care about yet still do.

Nina sends me a million messages to ask where I am and what's up with me tonight, but I ignore every single notification that pops up on my phone. At least, I ignore them until right before I go to bed, when my eyes fall on a message that just showed up.

Sierra Levine has left SMASHERS!, it says. That's all it takes for the world around me to finally come crashing down.

# 20. Never Let Someone Else Ruin Your Life

Apparently, when you cry yourself to sleep, there's a big chance you'll not only wake up with swollen eyes but also with literal dried salt sticking to your cheeks. Which is especially fun when the only reason you wake up is because someone decided to video-call you at eight in the morning.

I quickly rub my eyes and adjust my hair so it isn't too messy, but in all honesty, it's a lost cause. I take a deep breath and answer Veronica's call.

Her face appears on my screen, and I'm just about to greet her and ask what's up when she tells me, "Care to explain yourself?"

I blink in surprise. "Good . . . morning?" I attempt to say, but it comes out more like a question.

"Oh, don't look so innocent. I asked you to explain yourself," she repeats.

*Is she . . . angry?* I wonder, but the truth is, I can't read her face. I decide to go for the safest option and ask, "What happened?"

Immediately she snaps. "Jesus Christ, Eleanore, cut the

bullshit because we both know casual small talk is *not* why I'm calling."

*Right. Definitely angry,* I conclude.

Veronica pauses, then adds, "Sierra told me what happened last night, and I would like to give you the chance to tell your side of the story before I actually get mad at you. Because, trust me, this is not even a quarter of how angry I can get."

I think back to yesterday, to seeing Sierra at the party and feeling hopeful for approximately three seconds before everything fell apart. To seeing her push through the crowd in hopes of reaching the door as fast as possible. Then she was gone—so quickly that I couldn't even look at her face to see if she was worried, upset, or angry.

I've been wondering which of the three it could be—and more importantly, why—so much that my head hurts. Though that could also be because I've been crying my brains out.

"I genuinely don't know what you're talking about, Veronica," I try, which is the truth, but that only seems to anger her even more.

"Of course you don't." She shakes her head in frustration, looking away for a second. When she turns back to the camera, green eyes intense, she says, "Let me put it simply for you, then. I don't know what kind of ally you think you are, but you're doing an awful job at actually caring about people's feelings. Even *if* Sierra does have feelings for you, that doesn't make it okay for you to make your little friend tell her to stay away from you. She's not going to try and fucking turn you."

"Wait, what?" I freeze, a thousand questions entering my

head at once. What little friend is she talking about? And why would I ever want Sierra to stay away from me?

*This doesn't make any sense,* I tell myself before really thinking about Veronica's words. Slowly, the realization comes. *Did Nina actually . . . ? No, she wouldn't do that. Right?*

But as I think about it—about everything—there's no denying how the puzzle pieces click together perfectly.

"Oh. My. God," I say after a long silence. "Veronica, I— How could I be so *stupid*?!"

Veronica looks as confused as I felt only moments ago.

I take a deep breath, holding on to the hope that this is all some big misunderstanding. Carefully, I ask Veronica, "Did Sierra tell you anything else about . . . about what happened last night? Or even before that?" I ask.

She shakes her head, just like I thought she would, so I blurt it out: "Veronica, I kissed Sierra. At camp. I'm— I think I might be gay?" I add, but again, the uncertainty in my voice makes it sound more like a question.

Veronica frowns, that fiery anger still in her green eyes, but at least she doesn't snap at me this time. "Then how does that explain that during camp, you used Sierra as some kind of experiment so you could get back with your asshole of an ex-boyfriend?"

I let her words sink in for a second before cursing myself out, too.

*No wonder she's so mad,* I think. I'm half surprised she's even giving me the chance to explain what happened, because this all looks very, very bad for me.

Nina doesn't even know about our kiss, but if she really told Sierra I wanted to win back Daniel, then Sierra must've jumped to the conclusion that I used her. That all of it was pretend. I wish she hadn't been able to imagine I could do something so cruel, but I do understand why she believed it. After all, I was talking to Nina mere moments before the conversation happened, glancing at Sierra in a way that could've made me look suspicious.

I don't think I would believe in the good in me, either.

"Fuck." I sigh. Then I start at the beginning. Veronica doesn't interrupt me as I try to explain everything that happened during the past month. I tell her about my original plan to win Daniel back, about the deal Sierra and I made, about how I did ask Nina to talk to Sierra last night, and about how Nina must've taken that the wrong way.

How she told Sierra to leave me alone based on her homophobic assumptions.

*I should have realized,* I repeat to myself over and over again. *How could I not have realized?*

I know I probably already messed some things up with Sierra myself by not having the guts to reach out after camp ended, but at least that was *me* ruining things for myself. This is entirely different. This is the person who is supposed to be my best friend going behind my back to be awful in my name.

After I explain what I think happened, Veronica is silent for a few seconds. A few seconds during which I convince myself that she doesn't believe me and that both she and Sierra will hate me for the rest of eternity, but then she exhales. "Oh thank god." She clears her throat. "I would like to say I never once doubted you, but, well, I'm a pessimist, so . . . that would be a big lie. Either way, I'm just glad it's not actually true, because I am kind of really attached to you already."

Normally I would joke that that's the sweetest thing she's ever said to me, but I'm a bit preoccupied with trying to come up with a way to fix this mess right now.

"She's never going to talk to me again now, is she?"

"You don't know that," Veronica tells me. It's surprisingly positive for, well, Veronica. "She is really upset because of what happened, though, but at least she finally got confirmation as to who outed her last year. At least, pretty much."

I pause, frowning. "Hold on, *what*?"

"Oh." She clears her throat. "You didn't know about that yet? Well, you see . . . the reason Sierra wanted you to get Nina to talk to her is because she thought Nina outed her. They're neighbors, so Nina must've been able to see the pride flag in Sierra's room and told everyone at school. Sierra's been trying to confront her for ages, but she's been pretty hard to catch in private."

My jaw drops at that. For two reasons. First, it maybe shouldn't come as a big shock after everything, but it's still hitting hard that the person I considered my best friend would do such a hateful thing.

And second . . . "I assumed Sierra wanted to talk to Nina because she had a crush on her!" I exclaim.

Veronica flinches. "What? No! Ew! I'm offended on Sierra's behalf! Nina sounds like *the worst*!"

"Apparently she is," I whisper.

We're both quiet for a second before Veronica asks, "So . . . are you going to win back your girl now?"

I force the corners of my mouth to lift, but the smile falters with insecurity. "I'm going to *try*, yeah."

"Wow." Veronica studies my face. "You really, really like Sierra, don't you?"

A blush creeps up my cheeks. "I really, really do."

Veronica nods, and a few moments later, we say our goodbyes. My screen goes dark again.

I quickly send Sierra a message to ask if we can talk, but I honestly don't have a lot of faith in her answering me. Tomorrow, however, is the first day of our senior year of high school, and I know exactly what I need to do to show her I've learned from my mistakes.

First, though, I need to do the thing I've been putting off all summer: get myself to stop caring about what other people think of me. For real this time. No more doing things halfway—I have to choose between trying to please everyone all the time or simply living my own life.

It's time for me to truly choose the latter.

So, later that day, I do exactly what Noah has recommended I do for the past three years: I make a bonfire and throw my notebook into it.

Turns out he was right. Even if literally burning the notebook feels at least a little dramatic, it helps. As all the rules and lists and every single thing I let myself be held back by in that book goes up in flames, it's like I can breathe for the first time in a while.

I take a deep breath, letting the air go through my lungs as I relax . . . and am then launched into a coughing fit.

Okay, maybe this should've just stayed a metaphor, I think before I inhale even more smoke.

The point, however, is this: I have to let go of the life I've been leading for the past few years. Because as it turns out, I can't expect to be seen as the perfect, likable girl *and* be who I want to be.

It's a choice, and I know exactly what mine is now: I need to find my way back to who I used to be before other people's opinions got to me. The enthusiastic girl with the loud laugh who talked everyone's ears off. The girl who didn't care about what people thought of her, who didn't bear the weight of the world's judgment on her shoulders just yet. The girl who actually liked and accepted herself.

It's weird to admit this after all these years of locking her up somewhere deep inside me, but I think . . . I think I've missed that girl.

# 21. Desperate Times Call for Desperate Presentations

For the first time in the history of Mondays, I'm up before my alarm even goes off, which is a fun way of saying I didn't sleep at all last night. But hopefully that will all be worth it by the end of this first day of senior year.

Before I can get there, though, I have to survive my confrontation with Nina.

As soon as I enter school grounds, she's walking up to me, and even though I really do try to give her a hint by going in the opposite direction, she keeps coming until she's caught up with me.

"Can you believe we're actually seniors now?" she starts. Either she's pretending to not notice me ignoring her or she's actually oblivious. "God, I still remember when we came fresh out of middle school. The two of us were such weirdos." Nina laughs, shaking her head at the mere thought of it. "But look at us now! We made it!"

She studies me then, probably smiling at me expectantly, but I don't return her eye contact. In fact, I don't do anything but quicken my pace, jaw set.

Nina makes a surprised sound at that, as if she can't believe my audacity right now. "Okay, what the hell is up with you, Ellie? First you decide to randomly ghost me after your party, and now this? Is everything okay?" she asks then, and though I promised myself not to, I snap.

"You don't actually care," I say, briefly turning toward her.

A frown forms between her brows. "Now where did *that* come from?"

I cross my arms over my chest, stopping in front of the building where our first class will be starting in a few minutes. The only class I share with Sierra, Noah, Daniel, *and* Nina today.

"Guess," I tell her.

"I seriously wouldn't know!"

I nod, hating myself for being disappointed by her after everything that's happened. "That really tells me everything I need to know about you. Jeez, Nina, you're not even willing to admit what you said to Sierra to my face?"

At that, Nina tilts her head slightly. "This is about what I said at the party?" she asks, at which I mumble that "*Of course it is.*"

"I don't know if you somehow forgot or something," she starts, "but you're the one who asked me to talk to Sierra."

"To talk, yes! I wasn't asking you to—I don't know—*protect* me from her! She's not a freaking predator, Nina!"

"Um, that was heavily implied, though. I mean, come on,

Ellie, you should've seen your face! You looked like you were terrified of her and needed me to save you!"

A bitter laugh escapes me, the sound so unlike me that it shocks me. "You don't get to blame me for this. *You* were the one who jumped to conclusions. Ones rooted in homophobia, might I add, which you're not even willing to acknowledge. So no, I really don't want to talk to you right now. Please just . . . leave me alone from now on, okay?"

I start to walk away, but she still reaches for my wrist. "Don't be ridiculous. You're my best friend, Ellie," she tries one more time.

I take a step away from her. "Not anymore," I say, and it seems like the school bell loves a little drama, because it chooses this exact moment to ring. "See you around, Nina," I tell her, and then, just like that, I'm gone, finally on my way to a whole new chapter.

We're almost done with our first period of senior year when Mrs. Ahern finally puts me out of my misery.

"Now, as you all probably know, there's a little tradition here at Willowmoor High," she says, earning a few groans already, but I straighten my back. "Throughout your senior year, each of you will be expected to give a presentation in which you reintroduce yourself. I know most of you have been sharing classes with each other for years now, so it might seem a little strange to you, but it's a tradition for a reason.

"At the end of last year, you watched *The Breakfast Club* together. Does anyone remember what the central questions and themes were in that movie?"

It takes a few seconds for someone to raise their hand, but it's Noah who eventually helps out by saying, "The main characters are asked to write an essay about who they think they are, but instead of giving the answers that people expect from them, they refuse to be reduced to the boxes they've been forced into. They write their own stories."

Our English teacher smiles at him. "Exactly, Mr. Young. You've all changed so much since you first met, and yet you still see each other as the people you were at the start of your high school careers. With this presentation, we hope to give you the chance to show everyone who you are when there are no consequences, judgments, or expectations weighing you down. It's time for all of you to step outside of the boxes you were put in. Just like they did in *The Breakfast Club*."

Then Mrs. Ahern gets off her chair, making my heart rate spike even higher. "Normally, the first reintroduction wouldn't be until next week, but we have a very enthusiastic volunteer who would like to present today." Finally, her eyes land on me. "The floor is yours, Ms. Young," she lets me know.

There are murmurs all around me as I get off my chair. "What is she doing?" I hear someone say from behind me, but I don't turn around, instead trying to breathe evenly while walking to the front of the class. There, I quickly set up my presentation and turn to my fellow students.

Noah is giving me a little thumbs-up, and I find Sierra in the crowd, too, but she's looking everywhere except at me.

If all goes to plan, that won't be true anymore by the end of this presentation. So I take a deep breath and begin talking.

"If you ask anyone in this class who Eleanore Young is, I'm sure they'd be able to give you a clear answer," I start, scanning the familiar faces sitting in front of me. "She's that nice girl who almost everyone gets along with. A dream girl. One you can't imagine ever hurting somebody, even unintentionally, because she's far too sunshiny for that. Kind, happy, perfect—that's Eleanore.

"Now, I probably sound like I think a little too highly of myself, but these are all things that have actually been said about me over and over again, and if we're being honest . . . I'm not exactly proud of any of them," I admit, earning another few frowns. "Being the nice girl is always going to be a part of me, I hope, but it also reflects what I've been doing for the past three years: living my life for anyone but myself."

"What is she even saying?" I hear someone whisper, but I ignore them.

I take a deep breath before pressing a button, making the presentation behind me shatter into a million pieces to show a whole new slide. "It's time for me to stop trying to please everyone all the time," I say. It's a little dramatic, I know, but in my defense, it was past 3:00 a.m. when I decided to add this transition, so I wasn't exactly thinking clearly anymore.

"So who am I really, then, you might ask?" I continue, trying not to think about the way their faces will change once I get to the heart of this presentation. "The truth is, before this summer, I didn't know who I was, either, so all this is still very new to me, too. I have so much left to figure out, but thanks to the summer camp I went to last month, I now know more about myself than I ever did before."

I quickly glance at Sierra, who's fidgeting with her pen instead of paying attention to me. I swallow, then force myself to smile through my nerves. "At this summer camp, I got to know some lovely people who taught me a lot. Like how to love and accept myself and how to really open up to other people and, yes, even how to properly spike. It was a beach volleyball camp, after all." Nobody laughs at my joke, but still I go on. "All of this is to say that I've discovered parts of myself that I'm now finally ready to share with you. Because I'm not going back into that box of the Perfectly Nice Girl. I don't want to, and honestly, I *can't*. Not after this summer.

"So, here's the truth: I'm Eleanore Young. I'm seventeen years old and grew up in Willowmoor surrounded by a lot of the same people who are looking at me now, but no one except my brother, Noah, ever really got to know me. That changes now. In my free time, I like planning every single thing that can be planned, and yes, I'm also kind and supportive and thoughtful, because I know what it's like to be shut out thanks to the horrors of middle school.

"For the past three years, I had this list of rules that I followed to make sure none of you saw me as less worthy of your respect. To make sure none of you suspected I'm autistic . . .

which I am. I didn't want to be shut out again, so changing myself seemed like the safest option. It probably *is* the safest option, but I've decided it's time for me to take some risks, like telling you that this summer, while I was at camp, I fell in love with someone. Someone who's a girl, to be more specific. A girl who is so kind and amazing and who makes me feel like the bravest version of myself. I'm so ridiculously in love with her, and though I hope she feels the same way, even if she doesn't, I need her to know how much this past summer with her means to me."

I swallow down the emotion in my voice, looking around the classroom for a second. I'm answered with lots of blinking, and then . . .

"Damn! Good job, Daniel! You turned her into a freaking lesbian!" Oliver laughs, this being his only takeaway from all I've said so far. As was to be predicted. Mrs. Ahern tries to shush him, but the words have already traveled around the classroom, causing some chuckles.

I feel my body freeze for a second at Oliver's words, but then I smile, pressing the button again so it shows the next slide of my presentation. "Don't give Daniel too much credit, but yes. This summer, I discovered I'm a lesbian. I realized it's something I've always been but that I was so scared of everyone's judgment, I didn't let anyone know about this part of my identity—not even myself.

"But as you've probably guessed by now, I'm done suffocating parts of myself out of fear. I want all of me to be able to breathe, and I sincerely hope that you'll let me." I look some more people in the eye, including Nina. She looks like she's seen a ghost, her tanned skin suddenly very pale.

I resist giving her a bitter smile and instead continue with "So that's me. Eleanore Young. If you now find yourself thinking, *Wow, I actually don't know anything about this girl,* then you'd be one hundred percent correct. But I hope that from now on, you'll be open to getting to know me. The *real* me, not just the one you want to see," I say. "Thank you for your time."

For a moment, everything is completely silent as the entire class gapes at me, not knowing what to do. Including Sierra, who has finally stopped pretending not to listen but whose eyes I can't meet just yet.

"Should we clap?" I hear Michaela whisper to Katie, but before she answers, the bell rings, announcing it's already time for our next period.

And just like that, I walk out of the classroom, holding my head high because, for once, nothing is weighing me down.

# 22. Stay Close to People Who Feel Like Campfires

As proud as I am of myself for doing that presentation in front of everyone, it might not have been my best idea after all. Because I don't get a single chance to see Sierra for the rest of the school day.

I don't know if she's avoiding me or if it's because of our different schedules or, well, maybe it's both. The point is: She's nowhere to be seen, and I'm freaking the fuck out.

I slam my locker shut, a groan escaping me as I rest my head against it. "It's really over, isn't it?" I ask.

"Deep breaths, Ellie," Noah reminds me, leaning against the locker next to mine. "Even if Sierra doesn't want to be with you—and that's just an *if*—that doesn't mean it's all over. You grew so much this past summer, and that is something no one is *ever* going to be able to take away from you, okay?" My brother looks me right in the eyes. "Whether you get a girlfriend out of this or not, I'm proud of you."

I nod to myself, repeating his words in my head as I breathe in and out, in and out. “Thanks for staying here with me, Noah,” I tell him, giving him a smile that is at least partly genuine. “I think it’s time for us to go home, though.”

But my brother is now looking at something behind me. “Um, maybe think again, actually,” he says, and when I turn around, I understand exactly what he means.

Because pushing through the crowded corridor is Sierra Levine, as determined as ever. Her face might be completely blank and unreadable, but her steps are what give her away. Each one is taken with full confidence, in that same exact way she does when she’s on the volleyball court. When she knows exactly what she needs to do.

And this time, those steps . . . they lead her right to me.

If only I knew what that meant: Is she determined to kiss me or to kill me?

I can barely function by the time Sierra is standing in front of me, and my dysfunction only gets worse when she says, “We need to talk.” Then she grabs me by my wrist and drags me to the nearest empty classroom, ignoring the whistles coming from behind us. She simply locks the door, shutting out all the noise.

For a moment it’s completely silent.

“I can’t believe you!” she exclaims then, starting to pace around the room. “You can’t just go up there and give that speech only to disappear!”

I barely dare to move. “I had class,” I try, careful.

Sierra stops walking. “Not the point, Ellie. What I’m trying to say is that you can’t just . . . *confess* all that and expect me to be able to focus on math afterward! Seriously, this was the longest day of my life, and it's not even four p.m.!" She shakes her head at the mere thought. "Do you realize how hard it is to sit still and pay attention to what teachers are saying when all I want to do is run to you? To tell you that yes, of course I feel the same way?"

My breath catches in my throat at that. "Wait. You like me?" I ask, just to make sure I'm not completely delusional.

Sierra looks at me like I'm going to be the one to end her, not the other way around. "We really need to work on your confidence, but yes, I like you, Ellie. A whole lot," she confirms.

It's like a light spreads through my entire body instantly, filling every little hollow corner with warmth. As my heart beats its favorite rhythm in my chest, I smile my most genuine smile, not caring that Sierra can probably see every single one of my teeth right now.

"Awesome," I say. "I, um, yeah. If you didn't get the message yet, I definitely don't want what happened at camp to stay there."

The corners of her mouth lift into a smile. "I sure hope you don't, because I've been frustrated while waiting to do this all day," she says, and the next moment, her lips are on mine.

Finally.

We fall back into the rhythm we found at camp immediately, her hands on my waist and my arms around her neck. We're two flames of a crackling campfire, meeting in the middle until sparks fly all around us. Or maybe we're more like two waves, colliding with each other until you don't know where one ends and the other begins.

Whatever we are, Sierra and I fit together perfectly. Everything about the kiss is soft and slow, and I lose myself in her touch so completely that I forget we're still on school grounds.

That is, until the bell rings. *Loudly*.

I break the kiss, taking some time to breathe as heat rises to my cheeks even quicker than it did before.

After the bell stops ringing, silence fills the classroom as the two of us just breathe together. Once she's no longer out of breath, Sierra says softly, "You didn't have to lay your whole soul open for everyone to see during that presentation, you know. Like, you didn't feel pressured by me to come out or something . . . right?"

I shake my head, taking her hand in mine and squeezing it. "I wanted to, don't worry. And I actually did leave some things out of the presentation," I say. "I'm a demiromantic lesbian, so I only get romantically attracted to people after developing a strong emotional connection with them. I think that's part of the reason why I never realized I liked girls. I didn't let anyone into my life, so I was never really able to get crushes or—"

"First of all, you're rambling," Sierra interrupts, grinning as she takes a step closer to me. "And secondly, when did you realize all this?"

I press my lips together before saying, "I might've stayed up all night last night to research sexualities. The websites Maya sent me were especially helpful."

Sierra shakes her head and laughs. The sound fills my heart with warmth.

"So yeah," I continue. "This is all very new to me, but it feels *right*. It feels like . . . like *me*." I take her hand back in mine, and she squeezes it, just like I did to hers only moments ago, but because it's her doing so, my body basically stops working for a good three seconds.

*Focus, Eleanore.*

I clear my throat. "You're distracting me. What I'm trying to say is—I did leave some stuff out of that presentation, like how I'm still trying to work through years of trauma. How all of this actually terrifies me and I don't know if I'm doing any of it right but that I want to try. Because during those two weeks at camp, you didn't only teach me how to love and accept myself. Somewhere along the way, I learned to fall in love, too. And I did. With you."

She tugs a strand of hair behind my ear. "I guess we make the perfect team, then, Eleanore Young, because I feel the exact same way."

# Epilogue.
# Don't Be Dramatic . . . Actually, Do Whatever You Want

"THAT'S MY GIRLFRIEND RIGHT THERE!" I yell right after Sierra spikes, making the ball land right in the middle of the opponents' side of the court.

She turns around and jogs toward me, to a tall basket holding volleyballs. She uses the excuse of getting a new ball to tell me, "We're, um—we're actually just warming up right now, Ellie."

"I know," I say, not able to control the big grin on my face. "I just really like being your proud, supportive girlfriend."

She rolls her eyes at me but laughs. "You're insufferable."

I shrug. "You love me."

"Yes, I do. Those two statements can coexist." She glances back at the people behind her, then briefly returns her attention to me. "We are starting in a bit, though, so behave, please."

I simply give her a wink, watching as she walks back to her brand-new team. It took some work, but Sierra's dad finally decided to let her play indoor volleyball again after Gigi and I made David talk to him. It sucks that it took Adrian's old teammate to convince him of what his daughter wanted, but at least this way I get to see Sierra do what she loves.

It's not as ideal as when she played in Willowmoor, which meant she could bike to her practices, but Belford is not that far of a drive, either. Plus it gives me an excuse to meet up with Gigi and Sloane when I occasionally come along with Sierra, as Belford is their hometown.

I'm really not complaining about this change, though. The red Belford shirt looks *way* better on Sierra than the green one Willowmoor insisted she wear.

The time until the game really starts is ticking, so I quickly take my phone out of my pocket, rushing to type something to the group chat.

**YOU in A SMASHING! SURPRISE FOR SIERRA:**

WHERE ARE YOU ALL??????

Immediately I get a text back.

**LIAM in A SMASHING! SURPRISE FOR SIERRA:**

dude.

we were waiting for you to tell us we can come in?? we're literally right outside??

**YOU in A SMASHING! SURPRISE FOR SIERRA:**

oh.

well.

go ahead!

It's the most important game Sierra's had in a while, so I thought it'd be a good idea to bring her some moral support in the form of our camp friends. We haven't all been together since the end of this summer's edition of SMASH!, but I know it would mean a lot to Sierra, especially since, a while ago, she confessed she's still scared that the group only tolerates her because she was my friend at summer camp—and is now my girlfriend.

Maybe having all of them here, at *her* game, will make her realize they're just as much her friends as they are mine.

Her back is turned to the audience when Liam, Maya, Yasmeen, Sloane, Noah, Veronica, and Gigi all slip through the door. For some reason they're all overly careful not to make any sounds as they settle down.

The referee whistles to signal the start of the game, and so a still-clueless Sierra starts playing. It's only when she scores a point and has to serve that she turns around and sees us—all of us—in the audience.

She blinks for a few moments, as if she's convinced everyone being here is a product of her imagination. But it's not. This is real, and we're all here to cheer her on.

As she realizes that, her whole face lights up, that fire I like so much burning in her brown eyes again. And when she smiles at us, it's the smile of a winner.

Later that night, after the game and lots of catching up over dinner, we all go to Gigi's favorite park to continue celebrating Sierra's victory together. That's where we've been chatting for the past hour or so, some of us lying down in the grass while a few others have decided to claim a bench.

"There's something truly wrong with the weather these days." Maya says at some point, totally unprompted. "Like, it's the end of November! I should not be able to sit outside at nine p.m. without a coat!"

Noah hums in agreement. "The grass could also really use some rain. It's so dry, it actually kind of hurts to sit on," he says.

And barely five minutes later, of course, it *does* start raining.

"Dammit," I hear Veronica grumble next to me, followed by a million other curse words. I've got to give it to her: She's really creative when it comes to cursing. Impressively so.

It's the kind of rain that comes out of nowhere—one moment you can't feel a single drop, and the next your hair is being soaked as well as the fabric of your red winter dress, making it cling to your skin. The sensation of it is horrible, but as we all get up and look for a place to shelter, I know there's not a single thing I'd change.

In fact, while the rain pours down on us, I could make an

endless list of things I love about this moment. I love the way our laughs blend together, the sounds echoing through my entire body as my heart beats in a rhythm that feels like a warm home. I love that when I look to Sierra, her brown eyes are already on me. I love how her hand reaches for mine as we run through the streets and how we both slow down so she can pull me closer until, just like that, our lips fit against each other perfectly.

But the thing I love most about this moment and all the other ones that follow it?

They are mine.

# Acknowledgments

It's finally time for me to get sappy, so let me start by saying that *Smash or Pass* is a love story on many different levels. It is a queer romance novel and a book about friendship, and it includes two siblings who care about each other deeply, but at the heart of this book is Ellie, an autistic girl who learns to love herself. I sincerely hope that you, dear reader, felt that love while spending time with her at summer camp, but this love would not have been possible without the people who have made me into the writer and person I am today.

Thank you, first of all, to my incredible agent, Brent Taylor. I have truly found a literary soulmate in you, and I'm forever thankful to have you in my corner. Without your endless passion and sharp eye, this process would've contained much more self-doubt. (Yes, even more! Unbelievable, right?) Just as many thanks to Marisa DiNovis, my fantastic editor who saw the heart of this story when it landed in her inbox and offered it the home of my wildest dreams. When Brent called me with the news, I was making soup and not expecting to be starting such an amazing adventure with you by my side. Please don't pinch me, because I do not want to wake up!

Thanks are also due to the entire teams behind Knopf Books for Young Readers and Triada US Literary Agency, especially Lois Evans and Laura Crockett, who have championed this story in every possible way. I'm so, so grateful! Thank you to Rebecca Mock for the gorgeous illustration and to Michelle Cunningham for designing the cover. How do I even put into words how deeply I fell in love with it? I fear I can only offer you some loud squealing, if that's okay?

Then, to everyone I get to call my friend: thank you, thank you, thank you. I can't possibly list all of you (I'm really lucky to know so many great people!), but even if you're not in these acknowledgments, the love and support you gave me has been put into these pages. Miro, my summer camp best friend, who I dedicated this book to—who would've thought we'd still be here after all these years? I love you so much! Thank you also to Sage, Lian (is there anything gayer than putting your ex-girlfriend into your acknowledgments?), Mandy, Julia, and so many more. I couldn't wish for better friends! And, of course, to Isaak: You are the best thing that's ever been mine.

Thank you to the many (and I mean *many*) incredible writing group chats and communities I've been in, and the even lovelier people I met through those chaotic texts and Tweets. Thank you to Sophia Hannan for being the black house to my pink house, the green to my purple—you are insane and I love you beyond words. To Thea Liu, Wen-yi Lee, and Maddie

Martinez: What can I say except I'm really, truly Losing IT? And also to Kalie Holford, who means the world to me, and Sarah Underwood, who made me feel so welcome in the London author world, even though I don't live there. Can I say I love you a few more times?

Then, to the authors who took the time to read and blurb this book! I'm beyond honored to have your lovely words on both the back cover and pages of *Smash or Pass*. Especially Rachael Lippincott, who gave the perfect quote for the front cover, and to Rachel Lynn Solomon, my Amsterdam writing buddy, who is definitely way too cool to be friends with me!

And finally, to my family. (Warning: a bit of Dutch ahead!) Voor mama, my biggest fan and supporter from day one. Thank you for crying and cheering with me! I'm honestly so happy to have not only a mom but also a friend in you. Voor Bram en Toon, my brothers, who I love so dearly. I always look forward to your hugs and jokes! Thank you for everything. Voor papa—I hope you enjoyed your first romance novel, but if you hated it, please don't tell me because I really can't change it anymore! Jokes aside, though, I love you. Voor oma, opa, bomma, and bompa: I love you all to the stars and back. I wish I could fill more pages with these words, but my publisher probably wouldn't like that, so I'll just say it three more times: dank je, dank je, dank je! <3